WITHIN THE LIGHT

WITHIN THE LIGHT

KELLYANNE HALE

Charleston, SC
www.PalmettoPublishing.com

Paperback ISBN: 979-8-8229-4356-8
eBook ISBN: 979-8-8229-4357-5

ACKNOWLEDGMENTS

Although this is a fictional novel, many people from around the world have made this sequel possible. A simple "thank you" isn't adequate in expressing the gratitude I have for all of you who helped me complete this series.

Councillor Reid of North Ayrshire, Scotland, for your continuous support during this process.

My bestie Sue, for your continuous support and cheering me on!

Dale, for always willing to answer questions on the fly. Very much appreciated.

Dave, for providing Irish information. I had writer's block until you helped out.

Ms. Holly, for taking the time to tell the Gateside Inn history.

Auntie Irene's Café of Seattle, Washington, your lovely workers greeted everyone with a smile and made every patron feel welcomed.

Chapter 1

THEY'RE BACK!

A cold breeze shuddered through the stale winter air. It was not long before the news of the dead spread like a contagious disease and brought people from the far edges of Beith to see the ghastly sight. The dead stood in front of Agnes's house, unmoved by all the eyes focused on them. They stood with their eyes fixated on the front door, which was recently locked from the inside.

One woman who lived near Agnes thought she saw her grandmother. "Grandma. Is that you?"

Yet the elderly woman with three claw slashes on her face that looked like they came from a werewolf attack was undeterred. She looked at the woman, then slowly looked back at the front door. The woman was awestruck as she gasped in disbelief, holding her hand over her heart as tears flowed from her eyes. The woman backed away slowly while one of her friends tried to comfort her.

Surrounding neighbours brought warmer clothes for them to wear. It was challenging because their manoeuvrability was tautened, like dressing a mannequin from a clothing store. It was unclear if the dead understood what was happening, but luckily for the locals, the dead were nonviolent. Many others brought buckets of warm water and soap to try to wash away crusted old blood and the stale dirt the dead acquired clawing away from their graves. People still had funerals for their loved ones despite not having a body to bury. They needed a place to pay respects and remember loved ones, which many had spent decades grieving and eventually reached acceptance but were not fully at peace. Now seeing familiar faces from the grave, many hearts were torn open, reliving the horrific time of when the shadow took them. For many it was like a dull knife cutting them open, unstitching their partially mended hearts. No one believed this was even possible.

Inside Agnes's house, Anna and Thomas stood in the foyer. Anna was uncertain about where her room was, and Thomas, although he wanted to continue holding Agnes, had to let go and convey a dire message. They stood, continuing to greet each other with uncomfortable smiles, hugs, and odd gazes. It wasn't a moment later when Thomas broke his silence.

"Agnes, not many of us that returned are as lucid as Anna and me right now. You must know that the dead are here for you, and not in a good way either."

"What can I do to get you to stay?" Agnes asked. Once she saw Thomas in front of her, all she could think about was having her Thomas back. Her sweet Anna. If they had really returned, then they could be a family again. She looked at Thomas in desperation and love. Agnes went to hold him again, but he pushed her away. Thomas grabbed her upper arms, and with his eyes fully black, he exclaimed, "Agnes! Snap out of it! We are not here for you. We are not returning to you like we were! Vengeance is what the dead seek, and I would kill you myself if I didn't love you so much! What you have done is unimaginable, and your greed for power killed many. I am only here as a warning!"

Agnes stood silent. Rivers flowed from her eyes after hearing her beloved tell her he would kill her himself. She was stuck on that phrase and didn't hear anything else. Just then Anna's eyes turned black, her teeth became razor sharp, and she growled at Agnes.

"Mother! Death comes for you!" Just then the doors unlocked. Thomas let go of his tight grip on Agnes and walked slowly backwards, keeping his gaze on her. He turned slightly to open the door, and he and Anna departed. Thomas didn't shut the door behind him. It wasn't his house anymore, and it hadn't been since the shadow took him earlier that year. Agnes watched as they walked back to the group of the dead. She couldn't shut the door. Thomas and Anna were there, but even if she wanted to go to them, she couldn't go past her driveway, or she would likely be killed for sure.

Councillor MacDannels was starting to enjoy his lunch when he received a text with a short video attached. The text read, *Get down here now! They're all back!*

The video showed the dead standing in front of Agnes's house. Councillor MacDannels could not believe what he was seeing. He played the twenty-second video at least five times before he made the decision to head out to Agnes's residence. Surely Jessica McGowen would have this video in no time, and she and her crew would arrive sometime today. He had to think about where to put them. If anyone came into contact with them, they would be a priority for medical attention. The unknowns seemed limitless but needed attention now.

"Margorie, is the abandoned community centre still available?" he asked.

"Ah, yes, sir," Margorie replied.

"Good. I'm going to need that building opened as soon as possible. Meaning within the hour," MacDannels stated.

"What is this for, may I ask? Accommodations for much cleaning would be in order since it has been closed for over a year now," Margorie said.

"Let's just say it's not for a party, and a cleaning crew now is not a necessity. I will need a school bus down at Agnes Aird's place immediately," MacDannels exclaimed.

"Yes, sir," Margorie responded. She picked up the phone and made all the proper calls. Then she called Jeremy.

"Mum, you OK?" Jeremy seemed surprised to receive a call from his mum mid-afternoon.

"You and Christian busy?" Margorie asked.

"Ah, no. Why?" Jeremy asked.

"With haste please, go to Daniel's mum's house and see what is going on. I fear something bad has happened," Margorie said. Her voice was quiet because she didn't want others around her to hear her.

"It must be important because you're acting weird. Yeah, we'll go. I'll text ye if I see anythin'," Jeremy said.

"Thank you, love," Margorie responded.

Jeremy looked at his phone in bewilderment. He texted Christian. *Hey, my mum wants me to go to Mrs. Aird's house and see if something is goin' on there. You comin'?*

Sure, mate, Christian responded back.

It wasn't long before Jeremy and Christian arrived near Agnes's house. There were so many people on the street that they couldn't get through.

"What the bloody hell is goin' on here?" Jeremy exclaimed. He was amazed by all the crowds.

"Park there, mate," Christian said as he pointed to a nearby driveway.

"That is someone's house, you gommy," Jeremy said, while trying to manoeuvre his car to the driveway.

"I'm sure they won't care. They're lookin' too," Christian said.

They got out of the car and walked up to the owners, and Jeremy reassured them that they would only be there a short time.

"No problem, laddies. I hope Agnes gets her rightful death like she deserves," the elderly man said with conviction.

"Right. We're goin' to take a wee look and be right back," Jeremy said. Both thought the man was daft, but when they walked past the crowds and saw the dead standing there, their eyes widened in shock.

"Dude! No way!" Jeremy exclaimed.

"No way!" Christian facepalmed with his jaw dropped.

"I have to message Latrice. She's gotta have an answer to this shite," Jeremy said. He frantically texted her.

Hey! Get to Agnes's house now! You'll see when you get here, Jeremy messaged.

This doesn't sound good, Latrice replied.

You're right. It's not, Jeremy texted.

"Look! There's Agnes in the doorway. Let's go get a closer look," Christian said. Normally Christian was never that enthusiastic about anything, but this had him intrigued. Jeremy looked at him disturbed—his eyebrows raised and his face tweaked in a way to indicate Christian had gone mad.

"Oi. Let's go," Jeremy agreed. They moved through the crowds, and when they reached the house next to Agnes's, they stopped. Suddenly Jeremy's mobile alerted him of an incoming call. It was his mum.

"Well?" Margorie asked. The inflection in her voice indicated that she needed to know now.

"Ah, I don't know how to explain it, but it looks like those taken from the shadow have returned. They're standin' in front of Agnes's house. Not doin' anythin', just standin' there," Jeremy said.

"Well, the councillor and a bus are comin' that way to pick them up and take them to the old community centre. Do you recognize any of them?" Margorie asked.

Jeremy looked and saw Anna.

"I see Anna, but she doesn't look like Anna. Like she turned into something else. I don't know, Mum," Jeremy said. Just then it was as though Anna heard someone talking about her, and she snapped her head in Jeremy's direction. She growled at him with her razor-sharp teeth, then slowly turned her head to face Agnes's front door.

"Damn! Did you see that? We need to get the hell out of here!" Christian tugged on Jeremy to get back to the car.

"What happened?" Margorie asked repeatedly, before Jeremy would answer.

"Mum. It's definitely not Anna. She just growled at me, and she has razor-sharp teeth," Jeremy said.

"Sweetheart, come to my work," Margorie stated. She was scared for her son, and by the sounds of it, she had every right to be. Her heart was racing. Razor-sharp teeth? She couldn't handle the instant vision that came to mind.

"Mum. I'll be OK. Plus we have to wait for Latrice. Maybe she knows something about this," Jeremy explained.

"OK. I'm just worried for your safety. Please be careful and call me in an hour," Margorie said.

"OK. I promise," Jeremy said. They hung up, and just then vehicles were coming down the road, honking their horns. Jeremy and Christian looked towards the road and saw the councillor, his entourage, and a school bus. Jeremy now understood what his mum was goin' on about earlier. Behind them was Latrice, and she pulled into the driveway next to Agnes's house. The people standing there didn't think anything of it because they just thought she was part of the entourage. Latrice stepped out of her vehicle and walked towards the dead, but Jeremy yelled out to her, "Latrice! No!"

Latrice stood there. It was evident she was looking for her auntie, but she wasn't there. She had been eternally damned by committing suicide. Her reasoning was understandable, but higher powers that be thought she didn't deserve eternal rest. Latrice wanted to see her so badly. She walked in front of Agnes's house to get a different view. Then she saw Anna. Latrice tried not to show emotion, but there stood most of the dead. So many questions: How did they get here? Why are they not alive like the rest of us? Do they still have the shadow within them? Latrice knew the community would start looking to her for answers.

Councillor MacDannels looked at the situation and then began to speak to the crowd. "Everyone! Go back to your homes, please. We do not have the answers to this yet. However, we want to secure the situation as much as possible. We also don't want outsiders getting wind of this quite yet. I want to treat this situation with respect, but we also need to keep the community safe. Anyone with direct contact with the dead is to remain here for medical evaluation."

"That would have been only the murderer herself. Two of the dead came out of her house!" one neighbour said.

A few other people mentioned they helped clean and dress their loved ones.

Four people with positive-pressure protective suits exited the bus and surrounded the dead's lackadaisical formation. They motioned the dead towards the bus, but they stood still. This time all their eyes were black and focused on Agnes. Some growled, while some licked their lips and showed their teeth. It was as though they were motivating themselves before a kill. They could smell her, and they wanted to maul her to death. Thomas saw what they were doing and shuffled flaccid towards the bus. The mass noticed Thomas moving and followed behind.

"Where are you taking them?" one man asked.

"They will be down at the old community centre. I will make an announcement when it is safe to visit and acknowledge the possibilities as to why they are here," Councillor MacDannels said.

"We know why they're here. They want to kill her!" the man said. All eyes were on Agnes. Agnes noticed the dead, the neighbours, and the people staring at her in disgust. Councillor MacDannels couldn't have agreed more but had to keep his thoughts to himself. Her time was coming anyway. Soon she would be in front of the king and queen for her sentencing.

"Like I said. I will make an announcement. Thank you for your patience on this situation," Councillor MacDannels said. He rubbed his forehead and sighed.

His driver opened the door for him, and he quickly got into the back of the jet-black SUV. The bus followed the small convoy of vehicles, and people started heading back to their homes in anticipation of the councillor's announcement.

Agnes was in a daze as she shut the door and locked it. She slowly turned around and stared off into the distance. Her world had just been turned upside down, and she thought she had just entered a nightmare. Unconsciously she knew it was only fair, to say the least, for her to go through this pain. However, Thomas loved her still and had saved her life. Part of her wanted to die if she couldn't be with her Thomas and sweet Anna, but her thinking that was just crazy. She knew her sentencing from the high court would be soon, yet seeing them and not being able to be with them was torture enough. Agnes decided to call her sister. Irene was already preprogrammed in the monitor. She clicked a button from her remote, and the monitor pulsated, waiting for a connection. Irene answered but was not enthused to engage in conversation with Agnes. Irene was tired of being the middle person, intervening between Agnes and the kids and pretending to care about Agnes's current status. Irene's face appeared on the screen and had a blank look as if to say, *What do you want?* She decided to entertain what Agnes had to say with some courtesy and politeness.

"Agnes, how are you?" Irene asked, giving a slight smile. Agnes didn't answer. She stood there, looking at Irene, uncertain how to explain what she had just experienced.

"Goodness, Agnes! Out with it already!" Irene snapped, giving a snarling facial expression.

"Right. Thomas and Anna were just here," Agnes said. She was fidgeting with her hands, and her eyes shifted back and forth.

"Oh my. Your bum is oot the windae for sure! What are ye going on about?" Irene barked. This time she was about to just hang up on Agnes when Agnes calmly started to tell her what had happened.

"Irene, I swear that I'm not daft. It was the oddest thing. Almost all of those that were taken by the shadow returned in front of my house. They were dressed in long white, ankle-length robes and stood at the edge of the driveway. It was then when Thomas and Anna came in and warned me that they all want to kill me. The councillor just arranged for the dead, or whatever they are, to go to the old community centre. If you don't believe me, I'm sure Daniel can call one of his friends for confirmation," Agnes stated.

"So they're alive?" Irene asked.

"Not quite. They seem semi coherent, but death still fills them. Their eyes turn black, their teeth are jagged and pointed, and they growl. The only two I heard actually talk were Thomas and Anna," Agnes stated.

"The curse was lifted, and now all those that the shadow took came back?" Irene was intrigued and wondered if someone was using some powers from the black book.

"I guess," Agnes replied. There really wasn't a reason for them to return. Their souls should have remained where the shadow had taken them, according to the black book. Clearly those were lies. The shadow would do, would say anything to get souls for the dark king. Irene just sat quietly, covering each side of her forehead with her hands, looking down, then looked at Agnes.

After a few moments, Irene muffled a few words. "I don't know what to say. Keep me updated," she said, and she ended the call.

The screen went black. Agnes was certain now that not only did her husband want her dead, but so did the rest of her family. She had no one. Agnes covered her face and wept.

Jeremy and Christian followed Latrice to the community centre. When they arrived, they parked and saw the men in the protective suits graciously directing the dead inside. Latrice walked up to one of the men,

"Sir, how many are there?" she asked.

"We counted seventy, lass," the man replied.

"Thank you," Latrice responded. She saw the councillor get out of his vehicle and she ran up to him.

"Councillor—" Latrice started to say before she was interrupted.

"Ms. Beaumont, I am very happy to see you. Do you know what could have caused all this?" Councillor MacDannels asked.

"Well, that's why I'm here. If I could just try to talk with one of them, maybe it would give me clues on how and why they returned," Latrice stated.

"You would have to wear a protective suit. More importantly, I would be concerned for your safety. We have no idea what they are capable of, and quite frankly, they scared the hell out of the preventive medicine personnel. They have never seen anything like them before," Councillor MacDannels said.

"I don't think any of us have," Latrice said. She looked at him with concern.

"Are you OK, councillor? You look proper ill," she said.

"I'll be better once we know what to do with our past loved ones here. This is quite the delicate situation, and I need answers soon," MacDannels said.

"I understand. Please, let me try to help. The spirits will protect me." Latrice looked at the councillor with softness in her eyes. She, too, had made a promise when she became high priestess and knew this was one important way to keep that promise. He looked at her and was hesitant.

"I'm not liking the idea, but you are the closest we have to understanding what is truly going on here. OK, let's get a suit on ye and get ye inside," MacDannels said. He motioned one of the workers to bring her a suit.

"Thank you, Councillor," Latrice responded. She smiled. From a distance Jeremy and Christian observed the transaction between Latrice and the councillor.

"Oi, mate. What is she up to now?" Jeremy asked Christian.

"She's getting one of those suits. She's going inside!" Christian exclaimed.

"We have tae go with her!" Jeremy said. Christian rolled his eyes, and simultaneously they both got out of the car. They walked briskly towards the councillor and requested permission to go with her. To protect her, of course. The councillor agreed.

The building stood at the southeastern side of town. The long, wide driveway made of perfectly layered cobblestone led up to the small castle-like building made of grey brick and stone. Where once-luscious, perfectly manicured landscapes had embodied the thirty-five-acre lot, were now covered by intruding weeds and the overgrowth of clinging vines. The ground was covered with a light dusting of snow, adding to the building's eeriness. The centre of the building was an inner mini oasis surrounded by glass walls and a glass dome on top. This part had been added in the late nineteenth century to take away from the building's internal dreariness.

Latrice, Jeremy, and Christian entered the building and were guided towards a short hallway, then into the main room. Some of the dead got up and started roaming the premises, while others sat in the long, rustic wooden pews. Latrice motioned for them to sit down in the back. She quietly called out, "Anna. Anna's father." She paused, looked around, and didn't see anyone looking her way. She looked back at Jeremy and Christian. They whispered to her to try again, just a little louder. When she was about to speak, a man stood next to her with Anna trailing behind.

"Come. Follow me," Thomas said. Without saying a word, they got up and followed them to the musty old foyer near the entrance. There was one table set up, but because maintenance crews had arrived along with landscapers to prep the inner area, they would have to find another place to talk.

"Sir, if we can talk with our loved ones for a few moments before you begin, we would be much appreciative," Latrice said. The landscapers agreed and went back out the front to see what they could do there.

"Quick thinking, Latrice," Jeremy said.

"Well, I'm not going to let this opportunity go to waste," Latrice said.

. Latrice, Jeremy, and Christian slowly took off their protective headgear so Thomas and Anna could see them clearly.

"Hello. I am Latrice. These are my friends, Jeremy and Christian," Latrice started.

"I'm Thomas, father of Anna," Thomas said. His voice was coherent yet quavering. "I am glad you are here. I believe you are friends of my son, Daniel."

All smiled, nodded, and said yes. There was a slight pause, but Latrice knew she had to keep the momentum going, or she might lose them.

"Thomas, do you know what caused your return?" Latrice asked.

"That's a great question. All I know is that we were being tortured by demons and their animals, and the next thing we know, we are pushing our way through the dirt and gravitated towards Agnes's house," Thomas said.

Jeremy and Christian exchanged a strange look.

"Isn't that your house, sir?" Jeremy asked. Just then Anna's eyes turned black, and she growled at him. Thomas patted Anna on her knee and told her it was OK.

Jeremy's eyes widened, and he backed away a few feet. "I'm so sorry!" Jeremy exclaimed.

"The house is a very sore subject amongst us and the dead. Besides, Agnes is the one who sent many to their deaths through the shadow. There is no forgiveness for that," Thomas said.

"When you put it like that, I can totally understand, sir," Christian said.

"Please, call me Thomas. No need for formalities at this juncture," Thomas said, giving them a slight grin.

"How come the dead cannae talk, but you can?" Latrice asked.

"Another good question. I think it's because I haven't been tormented as much as the others," Thomas said.

"Why are the demons so determined to keep your spirit? What are they after?" Latrice asked.

"This is just a guess, but I presume they are after someone that caused us to go to the netherworld in the first place," Thomas said.

"Oh, I'm not going to say it. You say it!" Jeremy exclaimed to Christian.

"Um, no, I'm going to get growled at. I'm not an eejit!" Christian stated.

"Both of you stop it!" Latrice looked at Thomas, and said, "We are all thinking the same thing. If they wanted Agnes, they know where to find her. Why didn't the demons just go get her and let all of you go in peace?" Latrice asked.

Thomas chuckled at Jeremy and Christian, then he replied, "And that, lass, is the mystery."

Latrice was taken aback by his answer. She tilted her eyebrows down, turned her head to the side, and gave Jeremy and Christian a look of pure confusion. *What is he hiding?* Then she looked back at Thomas.

"You two were married. Knew everything about each other. Yet this is a mystery?" Latrice asked. This time it was more direct because she was determined to get an answer.

"I wish I could tell you more, but on this it's not clear," Thomas said. Anna was getting restless. She got up and started to shuffle along the grounds. "I better get her and settle her a bit. She was hurt the most, it seems."

"Thank you for all the information. I appreciate it very much. Me and my grove will do our best to do what we can to get you peace," Latrice said.

Thomas gave a smile, but in his own mind, he knew already there was nothing they could do. Their fate was inevitable.

Latrice, Jeremy, and Christian grabbed their protective headgear and headed out of the building, where Councillor MacDannels met them.

"Thank you, gentlemen, for giving us time," Latrice said to the landscapers. The gentlemen smiled and headed towards the inner sanctum.

"Councillor, this whole thing is a mystery. You have one person that is coherent enough to give us insight on what happened, yet everyone else seemed out of it. I will suggest that these individuals be treated with care and as delicately as possible. We were growled at just for the mere mention of Agnes's house. So I'm not sure what else would set them off. Bottom line, I'm afraid there is another mystery to solve."

"Thank you, love, for your detailed account. I shall make an announcement as soon as I can; however, I'm not looking forward to the news coverage that will follow," Councillor MacDannels added. He rubbed his forehead and headed back to his office, while Latrice, Jeremy, and Christian handed back the protective suits.

"OK, Latrice, I see your thoughts spinnin'. What are ye thinkin'?" Jeremy asked.

Latrice paused for a moment. She looked disturbed, then blurted out, "Why is Thomas hiding valuable information that could help him, Anna, and the rest of the dead have peace? There was a pact, all right, but there is someone else in this mix that no one is mentioning. At least, that's what I understood from Thomas's dialogue," Latrice exclaimed.

"I hate to break it to ye, but they're dead. They don't know the difference between the hole in their head versus the hole in the ground. We can't take what he or any of them say literally," Jeremy said.

"He sounded clear. Well, for the most part," Latrice said. Exasperated, she took a deep breath and shook her head in disbelief. "The whole thing just sounds off."

"Let's just take a break from it and discuss it more later," Christian said.

"Makes sense. Plus, I need to tell Daniel everything goin' on," Jeremy said.

"Actually, Daniel might be able to fill in the gaps on this mystery. The sooner he can come back here the better!" Latrice exclaimed.

"Checkin' out more books, are ye?" the librarian asked.

"I'm actually returning these," Sabrina said.

"You do have another book out, but you can keep that one," the librarian said. She looked at Sabrina and met Sabrina's gaze. It was as though they shared a surreptitious understanding that only they were privy to.

"Be safe and have a blessed Christmas if I don't see you prior to the holiday break," the librarian said.

"Thank you, and you as well," Sabrina replied.

As Sabrina walked by a group of girls sitting down, one of them whispered loud enough for Sabrina to hear, "There's the girl with the murderous mother. The one that cursed all of Beith for decades." She wore a devious smile that was coloured with plum lipstick.

Sabrina turned and leaned over the table directly in the girl's face, and said, "Watch yourself. I'll get my mother to put the curse on your house." Sabrina glared at them. She was fed up with the girl's constant remarks about her mother.

"I doubt that," the girl said. Then she pointed towards the telly. The running headline across the bottom of the screen read, *Agnes Aird Taken into Custody for Murder. Trial on Monday.*

Sabrina looked up, and her face instantly turned pale. The girl at the table continued to laugh. Sabrina turned and walked nimbly towards her locker. Tears flooded her face, ruining her eye make-up masterpiece. She tried wiping her tears away, but the black on her white uniform shirt just made things worse. She knew her auntie would be upset because of the shirt and going against her promise of not wearing make-up. Sabrina opened her locker and called her auntie.

"Auntie, can you please pick me up from school?" Sabrina asked while sobbing.

"Goodness, child! Is everything all right?" Auntie Irene said.

"I saw on the library telly that Mum got arrested, and the girls at school were being mean about it. Normally, I don't care, but this time just seeing it and hearing it from them just really hit me. Just please, Auntie, come get me, please. I'm already in enough trouble," Sabrina said. She knew she would face the consequences soon enough.

"Trouble?" Auntie Irene replied.

"You'll see when you get here," Sabrina said. She let out a soft sigh. Her day was already crap. Nothing she could do about it now.

When Auntie Irene arrived at the front office, she requested to sign Sabrina out of school. The secretary then asked the reason for the absence.

"It's none of your business, that's why. I'm her auntie, and I can," Irene said.

The secretary's eyes widened, and she just replied with "Yes, ma'am."

Sabrina walked out with her auntie, waiting for her "trial" to begin. They got into the car and just sat there. It was quiet. After a few moments, Irene spoke pleasantly and lovingly to Sabrina. Irene turned to her and said, "Sabrina. I am so sorry all this is going on with your mum and those little brats at school." Sabrina smirked. "To say that you just have to put on a brave face and just deal with it is partially true but also not helpful. You have to talk about it. I'm not saying we have to see a psychologist, but talk to me or Daniel or even your best friend. You can't let it fester and control your thoughts."

"I know. I'm just embarrassed. No one around here understands about the curse in Beith other than what they hear on the news," Sabrina said.

"Then maybe it's time to tell your best friend. Start there. She's a lovely lass and loves you as a dear friend. She's always asking how to help," Irene said.

"OK. I will. Thanks, Auntie." Sabrina smiled.

"Now, on the matter of your make-up. No make-up for a week for disobeying me. Yet I realise you are not a wee yin anymore. We will come up with a compromise, and when we do, I don't want a fuss. I want to be able to trust you. Make sense?" Irene said. Firm but gentle as well. Irene was not only the auntie, but her role was also mum and, in this instance friend.

"Yes, ma'am!" Sabrina said, grinning from ear to ear.

Chapter 2

THE TRIAL

Laurie froze, and just then pieces of her slowly started to break away and drift above her. The screams became louder and louder.

Daniel quickly sat up in his bed, sweating profusely and breathing erratically. He shut his eyes for a moment, breathed in, and let out a long sigh, realising it was only a nightmare. The same one that had kept reoccurring since that painful day when he lost his love. The day he lost everything else. Daniel moved gradually towards the side of the bed, still trying to calm himself from the nightmare, and while rubbing his eyes, his mobile buzzed. It was a text from Jeremy.

You 'round, mate? It's important!!!!!!!!! Jeremy texted.

Daniel rolled his eyes a bit. Jeremy would say things many times before and say something was "important" that really wasn't. However, Daniel humoured the idea that it was important, considering the number of exclamation marks Jeremy had placed in the text.

Humour me. What's goin' on? Daniel replied.

Just then a rhythm of bells for a ringtone chimed, and it was Jeremy calling.

"Well, now! It must be important." Daniel chuckled.

"You're goin' to want to come back to Beith! Like now, mate!" Jeremy stated. It was the shakiness in his voice that concerned Daniel.

"OK, you have my attention. What's goin' on?" Daniel asked.

"Daniel. You are going to think I'm absolutely doolally, but I swear it's true!" Jeremy took a deep breath, then continued. "The people that were taken from the curse have come back to kill your mum. But they are at the community centre, and Latrice talked to your dad and sister."

Without hesitation, Daniel yelled, "You think this is some kind of joke? After everything I have been through, that's the best prank you can come up with? That's pretty low, Jeremy. Even for you!"

"I understand how this sounds. Trust me! But I'm not lyin'. You can message Latrice. She talked with Anna and your dad. Mate, like I said, you just need to come back to Beith," Jeremy was calm at this point. He knew this would not go over well with Daniel, and if Daniel did come back to Beith, Jeremy wasn't sure how Daniel would handle the current situation.

"Let me talk to my auntie. I'll text ye later." Daniel clicked the end button and couldn't make heads or tails of what he had just heard. He sat there, shaking his head, thinking, *No way! No way!* The reason he had left Beith was to get away from it all so he didn't have to face it again. Yet the feelings, like crashing ocean waves, were drowning him. Daniel missing Laurie, possibly seeing his sister and his father no less became too much to embrace. He had to muster the strength to confront them and just accept the challenge that had been given. Daniel wasn't sure he was ready, but a part of him knew it was time.

He got ready and packed a bag, presuming he would stay at Jeremy's house for at least a few days. Daniel went downstairs to address his auntie.

"Hey, Auntie. Have you heard from Mum?" Daniel asked. His tone was casual to suggest he was unaware of the goings-on in Beith.

"As a matter of fact, I have. I didn't think you wanted to talk with her," Irene said. She glanced at Daniel's shoulder and noticed a heavy backpack. "Are you planning on going somewhere?" she asked.

"Going to hang with Jeremy for this week," Daniel stated.

"The heck you are! I forbid it!" Irene demanded. Daniel looked at her with pleading eyes.

"Auntie. I know what's going on in Beith. If this is a chance for resolution and peace, I'm willing to accept what pain comes with it," Daniel said.

"Oh, sweetheart. You will see things that are not what they seem. Your father and sister are not truly your father or sister. You do realise that, right?" Irene said. Her heart was racing, and she wanted to plead with him to not go.

"I just don't want you to get hurt, physically or mentally," she added. Daniel gave a slight smile and appreciated her understanding and love. He knew that she understood she could not stop him from going. "You must finish your finals first. Then you can go for as long as you need. I know there is much going on there now, but you need to be patient," she said.

"Crap! You're right. Plus I have a rugby game," Daniel replied. "I gotta text Jeremy and let him know. He's been going rocket because I won't come to Beith today." Daniel rolled his eyes, insinuating Jeremy's constant overwhelming emotions. Daniel's mobile rang again. No surprise it was Jeremy.

"I was just about to text ye. I'll be there Thursday, the twelfth," Daniel said.

"Thursday? Thursday?! We need you now!" Jeremy yelled.

"Goodness, mate! I have finals and a game! Everything will be fine. Just talk to Latrice and make some next steps to handle this so we will have a plan when I get there. OK?" Daniel said. He knew he had to negotiate a plan for Jeremy to agree to, to keep his mind occupied until he arrived.

"That's a brilliant idea. OK, see you on Thursday," Jeremy replied.

"If there is something else that happens, just keep me informed," Daniel said.

"Will do," Jeremy said. Then there was a dial tone. Daniel was relieved that he was able to calm Jeremy down for a little while at least. The mobile rang again. It was Jeremy.

"Oh my gosh, dude. What?" Daniel laughed.

"You might want to turn on the telly," Jeremy said.

Daniel, without asking why, just flicked on the television and saw that his mum was being arrested. He sat there emotionless, yet memories of how they would joke together swooped in. She would always be in the kitchen cleaning, making tea or bread, or fussing over the family.

"Ye there, mate?" Jeremy asked. Jeremy didn't want to sound too frantic.

"Yeah. I'm here," Daniel replied. His voice was certainly mellow in tone.

"You goin' Monday?" Jeremy asked.

"Nope. Plus, I have an exam on Monday. I'm sure it will be blasted on the news," Daniel said. His nonchalant demeanour wasn't a surprise to Jeremy, but he had to ask.

"OK. I'll leave you be. Or maybe I'll call back in ten minutes. Not sure yet," Jeremy said jokingly.

"Bye, you numpty!" Daniel laughed. He hung up and shook his head with a big smile. He could always count on Jeremy for that.

Dreariness draped over Beith like a moth-eaten blanket. Some of the locals were jubilant; some were uncertain if Beith was truly safe since the dead's return. One thing was certain: Agnes was going to meet the king and queen, to seal her fate. Many of her neighbours cheered for joy as the police picked up Agnes from her residence. It would be the last time Agnes could wear regular clothes before her judgement. Her hair was wavy; she wore black trousers, a black and white blouse with thick vertical stripes, and flat black leather shoes. She didn't bother putting on make-up or wearing any jewellery because neither was permitted in prison. Plus, any jewellery would likely never be seen again once she handed her personal items to the guards. Agnes thought about the earrings her sweet Anna had made for her. Agnes remembered wearing them for the first time. Gold with dangling rubies. A small smile lit Agnes's face. The smile quickly faded as she noticed a large group of protestors at the edge of Beith's city limits. They held large signs that read *"Kill her!" "Liar! Liar! – Set her on Fire!" "Beith is better without her!"*

As the vehicle got closer, Agnes recognized many of the protestors, and one woman in particular was Nancy. Agnes locked eyes with her. Nancy was holding a sign that read, *"Kill Her!"* Normally the officer wouldn't talk to the prisoner, especially right before a trial, but he couldn't hold back after seeing the protestors.

"I've been a police officer for five years now and have never seen this much angst against a person. You definitely deserve the title of 'Mother Murderer,'" the officer said.

"Shut up, mate. She might send her demons to snatch you and send you to hell!" the other officer stated.

"Piss off!" the officer driving said.

Agnes didn't even have those powers when she was free let alone now. Every bit of hate towards her, although deserved, felt like daggers piercing her body. Her sanity slowly drained like blood from each verbal stab. The torment might subside over time, but it didn't matter. Time to herself was all she had. Even the current torment wouldn't keep her company for long. Soon Beith would forget about Agnes. The ignominious fame from news reports would dissipate, and all that would be left was her physical form. Nothing about her would matter to anyone.

Agnes shrugged off her thoughts and held her head a little high. Soon she would arrive at His Majesty's high courthouse of Glasgow. Below the courthouse was a temporary, high security jail where new arrivals were taken only if there were accommodations readily available and their hearing was within the week. There Agnes would be stripped of her civilian clothes and put in a tan jumpsuit with a prisoner number.

King Andrew II and Queen Cara remained in Glasgow to carry on traditions as governed by King Andrew I. The castle in Edinburgh was revered as the castle of the beloved Mary, Queen of Scots, and they vowed her legacy should be known for generations to come. Both their majesties felt unworthy to occupy the renovated Edinburgh Castle and had a more modern castle made that closely mirrored Newark Castle. The L-shaped, off-white brick castle was two stories high. On the roof, at each of the far ends, stood square turrets or watch towers, and the parapet walks were filled with solar panels.

Each tall window on the first floor opened out to a beautiful attached curve-bricked flower bed that in the spring was filled with pink, white, and yellow flowers. The second-story windows had the same array except for the queen's lounge room. That particular room had her own private covered balcony facing the Clydesdale River. Upstairs there were five bedrooms, three full baths, the queen's lounge room, and the king's chamber.

Downstairs was the formal dining room and two large sitting rooms—one for formal gatherings and one for family entertainment. At the far west side of the castle resided the staff, seventeen members that included the cooking, cleaning, and grounds-keeping crews, as well as security, a butler, and the queen's handmaid. The queen herself ensured everyone, except security, knew how to fill in staff roles when others went on holiday or someone became ill. Displayed in the kitchen were the most modern stainless-steel appliances and cookery. Just outside was a greenhouse filled with herbs, vegetables, and a few berry bushes. Off to the north was a brick stable with a cone roof that housed horses, goats, and cows.

People were welcome to enter the grounds where the nursery was located near the river in the spring and summer to walk and have picnics. The Scottish people admired the king and queen for their down-to-earth demeanour, their care for the people, their abundance of charity work, and their proper policies to govern the country. It was not always white picket fences and red roses, but nevertheless, Scotland was at peace.

December 9, 2080—the day of reckoning for Agnes.

News crews from around the United Kingdom smothered the streets of Glasgow waiting for a verdict. One newscaster, Jessica McGowen, was front and centre, making her presence known before the courthouse.

"Can you hear me now, John?" Jessica asked. The newsroom wasn't picking up her signal earlier.

"Yes, we can hear you now," John said. A huge screen behind where he was sitting zoomed in on Jessica's face.

"Brilliant! I am right here in front of His Majesty's grand courtroom for the moment many from Beith have been waitin' for," Jessica stated.

"What is the atmosphere like there surrounding the possibility of a guilty verdict and a possible death penalty?" John asked.

"Excellent question, John. I have spoken to a few people here, and they are all for the death penalty. What is important here, John, is that this will be the first murder trial that the king and queen will attend, and they could possibly overturn a death sentence if the judge chooses that route," Jessica stated. "I'm going to have the camera zoom in over here. As you can see, many people are holding signs stating 'Kill her' and 'An eye for an eye!' Many from Beith have been here since early this morning waiting for the proper verdict. Back to you, John."

"Thanks for that report, Jessica. All eyes on Agnes Aird for the murder conviction and sentencing," John said.

Inside the courtroom was the grand court chamber. The chairs and tables were made out of country pine wood with purple velvet seat covers. There were five sections: the first was the Judge's seat, which was the largest in the chamber. There were two rows in front of the Judge's seat, which sat six on each side for the council members. The next two sections were reserved for the procurator and defence teams, which sat four on each side. The last section was the balcony, which was for immediate family, witnesses, and victims. The king and queen sat in a separate enclosed balcony off to the right of the judge. Spectators, news reporters, and the like were prohibited from entering the chamber; therefore, three cameras were situated behind the judge—one at the far end on each side of the wall and one in the centre.

This morning, Agnes already knew it was her fate to receive the guilty verdict, but would she be the first woman to get the death penalty? The death penalty had been reinstated in 2078 for those most heinous crimes, such as murder and child rape. Agnes definitely fit into the murder category. She would also have the choice of firing squad or lethal injection, or the judge would choose for her.

Her cell door rolled open, and two female guards cuffed and shackled Agnes's arms and ankles. They transported her to the prisoner tube where she was sent up, like on an elevator, to the main chamber's left side. Two guards promptly grabbed her and removed the ankle shackles and escorted her to the prosecution desk, where one of the guard's remained behind her.

Agnes looked around and watched as witnesses from Beith filled the balcony. Councillor MacDannels sat down and looked at Agnes with a disheartened look. Judy and Latrice sat down next to him. Agnes caught Judy looking at her, and she smiled, but Judy didn't reciprocate the expression.

One of the councilmen stood at the right side and announced the arrival of the king and queen.

"All rise! King Andrew II and Queen Cara have entered the chamber!"

All rose and bowed in the royals' direction.

Today was not the time for tiaras and crowns. King Andrew II, nephew of King Andrew I, stood a towering 182 centimetres; he had very broad shoulders and was muscular. He had brownish-blond hair and, uniquely, one green eye and one blue eye. His goatee was properly trimmed and maintained. He remembered his uncle briefly mentioning a Druid he once knew that had turned to the dark side of things. Hence, King Andrew II was intrigued by this particular case.

Queen Cara, born and raised in Ireland, had caught the king's eye when they met at an art gallery in Edinburgh. Princess Cara at the time visited Scotland often to escape the political idiocy of whether or not Ireland should have royalty representing Ireland. The thought of it would remind the people of King Archibald and his immature and belligerent attitude. Fifty years later, after he was stabbed, he still hadn't changed.

However, Queen Cara wasn't like that at all. She was warm and giving and had a heart of gold and the beauty of a goddess. Her long, wavy brown hair and her sea-blue eyes mesmerized those who looked at her. She had married the king in 2075, and they had been the best leaders of Scotland since the Beloved Queen.

As the king and queen chatted amongst themselves, the procurator fiscal team arrived and situated their notes upon the desk and remained standing with stern facial expressions. It was as though they knew the case personally and whatever evidence they presented would grant them victory. That victory would be the death penalty. Agnes glanced their way and knew they were out for blood. Yet no one in Glasgow, Edinburgh, or anywhere in Scotland would understand why she had tried to protect her daughter. The grove as well. Yet none of that happened. Agnes was now at the judge's mercy.

The councilman stood below the royals' balcony and announced the judge.

"All rise! The Honourable Tyler Maxwell resides over criminal case #600132. Agnes Aird versus Beith, North Ayrshire, Scotland."

Judge Maxwell was a tall, slender man of 178 centimetres, with jet-black hair cut short, a moustache that curled slightly, and brown eyes and wore circular-lens glasses. He always walked as though something highly pressing was happening, and he couldn't be bothered. It was intimidating to look at him, especially in his black robe.

His seat had the most elaborate décor on the back top, country pine wood carved to show a lion, a gryphon, and a thistle, representing the king, justice, and Scotland.

The cameras in the courtroom turned on, and the Judge Maxwell addressed the room.

"Your Majesties, councilmembers, witnesses, victims, and family. Thank you for your attendance. This will not be a long, drawn-out case; however, never in my fifteen years have I seen a case like this. I am not well versed in the ways in Druidism, but I'm quite certain the way you represented this religion, Mrs. Aird, is an abomination. You have been charged with seventy-five counts of murder, which includes your husband and underage daughter, by using undetermined outside forces, using protected land for these undetermined outside forces to assist in the murders, and disobeying the laws of His Majesty, the King, to report the known location of an altar. How do you plead?" Judge Maxwell asked.

Agnes stood up, and her handcuffs clanged on the desk, and the cameras zoomed in on Agnes's face. Then she replied, "Guilty, Your Honour." She knew she was guilty and that there was no way to alter the verdict.

Judge Maxwell now asked for any victims, witnesses, or family members to speak to the accused.

"Ladies and gentlemen, are there any members in the balcony that would like to address the accused?"

"I would, Your Honour," a young lady said.

"Granted. Guard, escort the young lady to the podium please," Judge Maxwell said.

As the young lady approached, he asked, "Please raise your right hand. Do you swear to the Almighty God that you will tell the truth, the whole truth, and nothing but the truth?"

"I, Judy Lochland, do swear to the Almighty God to tell the truth, the whole truth, and nothing but the truth," she responded.

"How do you know the accused?" Judge Maxwell asked.

"Your Honour, I was in her grove. She was my high priestess," Judy replied.

"Very well. Continue with your statement," Judge Maxwell said.

"Your Honour, Your Majesties, I am here not to plead for a lesser sentence for Mrs. Aird but merely to give a brief testament of the Druid ways and possibly the reason for Mrs. Aird's actions," Judy started.

"We don't have time for that now!" Judge Maxwell snapped.

"Honourable Maxwell, this information could prove crucial and give the community an understanding of Druid ways. Something we could all learn from. I would like to hear what she has to say," Queen Cara said. Her response was polite with a touch of demand. She had a way with words, and it was probably not wise to disappoint the queen. The Honourable Maxwell paused for few moments before speaking again.

"I will allow it. Please proceed," Judge Maxwell reluctantly said. However, he said it in a manner that made it clear that he'd made the decision himself. The king and queen could make suggestions but not decisions in the courts.

"Thank you, Queen Cara." They exchanged a smile. "Thank you, Your Honour. Being a Druid is being peaceful with nature, yourself, and others. We are grateful for the spirits of the earth and sky providing us with guidance and wisdom to live out our Druid ways. We rely on a high priest or priestess to talk directly to the spirits and accentuating our roles as an ovate or bard. I am an ovate. Honestly, I'm more known as the cheerleader who keeps the grove motivated. Now about Mrs. Aird, I overlooked something that I probably shouldn't have because I have spent much time justifying or defending her actions. Normally I am the one that sets up the table with the chalice, but on the day of Latrice's initiation, it looked like someone had already completed the set-up. So when a person is wanting to enter the grove, the spirits have to grant them access by fire or deny them by ice. When I went to check the set-up, I noticed a device that the chalice was placed on and wiring that led to the firepit. When I asked her what it was, she looked just as shocked as I did. When we asked the spirits for their guidance and decision, it took the spirits longer than usual to accept Latrice into the grove. Another instance was at the jubilee when we realised that Agnes had something to do with the shadow. Her reaction when the shadow snatched Anna was just out of touch. Bottom line, she didn't have the blessing from the spirits, no power, so she chose to make a deal with a demon. What little power she thought she had, she thought she could use to protect her family and the grove," Judy stated.

"Why didn't she stop after the deaths? Especially the death of her family?" the queen asked.

"Mrs. Aird, answer Her Majesty, as this can only be answered by you," Judge Maxwell demanded. Agnes stood up and faced the queen.

"At first I thought I had control of the situation. Then I knew I would lose my high priestess status if I told the truth about my lack of powers to commune with the spirits. It was out of selfishness, Your Majesty," Agnes stated. Her voice trembled a bit, but she still maintained her composure.

"Damn right it was!" Nancy said. Nancy had to see for herself what would happen to Agnes.

"I WILL HAVE ORDER IN THE COURTROOM! ORDER I SAY!" Judge Maxwell yelled. Nancy was lucky she wasn't deemed a spectator and removed from the courtroom. He regained his equanimity and addressed Judy.

"Is that all, miss?" Judge Maxwell asked.

"Yes, Your Honour," Judy replied.

"Thank you for your statement. You may return to the balcony," Judge Maxwell said. He continued, and asked, "Is there anyone else that would like to speak on the accused's behalf?"

The only thing heard at that moment was a pen someone was tapping on a notepad. The cameras scanned the room, but everyone remained silent.

"If there are no other statements, Procurator Fiscal, you may give your closing statement," Judge Maxwell directed.

"Your Honour, Your Majesties, and councilmembers, Beith has waited fifty years for this liberation of freedom.

Innocent lives lost, including her husband and daughter, and at what cost? To give her special powers to control a religious group? The facts are these powers never existed, and she worshipped something that caused death. Period! Even after years of this 'demon' taking lives, she continued to allow it to happen! Did she try to stop it? No! The accused openly admitted that it was out of selfishness. This isn't an insanity case where 'the devil made me do it'; this is a murder case. The only sentence based on our laws is the death penalty. Thank you," the procurator stated. He bowed to the royals and sat down.

"The defence may give their closing statement," Judge Maxwell said.

"Your Honour, Your Majesties, and councilmembers, Mrs. Aird did not directly murder each of the innocent victims. She didn't go to each resident and murder them. We do not know much about the Druid religion, but we have learned that it is peaceful and doesn't murder or destroy living things. Druidism has been in her family for generations, and she doesn't know any other way to protect than through the spirits. Mrs. Aird knew she didn't have much spiritual powers and used other means to try to protect her grove and her family. Unfortunately her intentions had negative consequences. Based on our laws, we recommend twenty years to life. Thank you," the lawyer concluded.

"Based on the confession from the accused, the witness statement, information from Beith's councillor, and closing arguments, we will adjourn to our chambers for review," Judge Maxwell determined.

"All rise!" the councilman said.

All stood until Judge Maxwell and the councilmembers left the chamber.

Latrice and Judy were quietly bickering amongst themselves.

"Are you kidding me? You can't just ask her?" Latrice exclaimed.

"Watch me!" Judy glared.

"Your Majesty, the queen. I would like to request an audience with Her Majesty in reference to Beith and remnants from the curse," Judy stated. She stood proudly and knew she could be arrested for addressing the queen, but she took that chance. Latrice did a facepalm and felt like Judy was going to go to prison.

"Talk to her now. If there is more to this curse and demon madness, we should know so we can stop it," the king stated.

"Guards. Please escort the young ladies to the meeting room," the queen stated. The queen had noticed the two talking and knew something important needed to be conveyed. They met just outside the room. Judy and Latrice did a proper curtsy to the queen, and then the guards opened the doors.

"Please wait outside and alert me when they are ready for sentencing," the queen said politely. The guards nodded and closed the doors.

"You are very brave. If the Honourable Maxwell would have heard you, he would have held you in contempt of court or gone overboard on something." The queen chuckled a little. "The king is intrigued, and frankly so am I. Please, sit and tell me briefly what's happening now in Beith."

Judy's eyes lit up, and she excitedly explained, "Your Majesty, once we found that altar and destroyed it, the curse seemed gone, but all the dead came back!"

"OK, maybe not that brief. What do you mean the dead are back?" the queen inquired. Her eyes were now widened, and she became very nervous.

"Well, last week—" Judy started.

"The dead have been around for a week?" the queen exclaimed. It was more of a loud whisper because she didn't want outsiders to hear.

"See why I requested an audience, Your Majesty?" Judy replied.

"Yes, continue." The queen sighed.

"Last week, the dead, wearing torn white robes, rose from their graves. People still had funerals for them even without bodies. Apparently once the curse was lifted, the graves were like portals back to us. They staggered towards Mrs. Aird's house, then just stood there until the councillor arranged to get them to the community centre. The councillor thought that would be the best place until medical staff could declare the situation safe," Judy explained.

"Your Majesty, I talked to Thomas, Agnes's husband," Latrice added.

"The dead can talk?" the queen exclaimed.

"Well, Thomas is the most lucid and seems to be, in a way, the leader," Latrice said. Her voice heightened at "leader." She continued, "I assessed he is judicious because he wasn't tormented like the others and was able to talk with Agnes prior to going to the community centre."

"Why wasn't this mentioned in court today?" the queen asked.

"Your Majesty, we believe that it has nothing to do with this particular case. That there is something more malevolent happening," Latrice replied.

"Hmm, Druids," the queen said. She was thinking out loud. Latrice and Judy looked at each other in befuddlement.

"Your Majesty?" Latrice asked.

"My sister in Ireland is a Druid and could probably help," the queen suggested. She took out a pen and some paper from her Ellen D'nor purse and wrote out her sister's information. Then she continued. "I ask that you don't give this to anyone. My sister lived in my shadow for years. She's happy doing her thing without being known as the 'queen's sister.'" There was a pause because the queen missed her sister immensely. Only time would tell when they would see each other again. She brushed off her thoughts and smiled at Judy and Latrice.

"We give you our word, Your Majesty," Latrice and Judy stated simultaneously.

The queen smiled. There was a knock at the door. The door opened.

"They are ready, Your Majesty," the guard said.

"Thank you," the queen said. "And I thank the both of you ladies for the information."

Judy and Latrice got back to the balcony. When the queen sat next to the king, he immediately addressed her.

"More madness, I presume?" the king asked.

The queen raised her eyebrows and gave him an expression that said there was definitely more to discuss. She retorted, "Oh my."

"Oh dear," the king said. He knew by her look that this wasn't truly over.

"All rise! The Honourable Tyler Maxwell has entered the chamber. Remain standing for the sentencing," the councilmember stated.

"As mentioned before, this case has brought unknowns, and we must address them in this case and any future cases. We must also understand that cases like these are not cut from the same cloth as other murder cases, and we must treat such notions in a delicate manner. Mrs. Aird, you have been found guilty of seventy-five counts of murder, which includes your husband and your underage daughter, by using undetermined outside forces, using protected land for these undetermined outside forces to assist in the murders, and disobeying the laws of His Majesty, the King, to report the known location of an altar. Normally I would present sentencing guidelines as they would pertain to this case; however, due to the nature of this case, no sentencing guidelines have been established. Therefore, based on the evidence, statements, and closing arguments, I impose the sentence of life in prison without the possibility of parole. Guards, please take the prisoner to her holding cell," the Honourable Maxwell said.

The second the judge announced the sentence, Mrs. Aird's whole demeanour changed. She was no longer Mrs.

Aird or Agnes, she was a prisoner, as though she didn't have a right to her own name anymore. As the guards escorted her to elevator, she glanced towards the balcony. Judy, Latrice, Nancy, and Councillor MacDannels were already gone. No last smile or a wave goodbye. No family present to give her one last hug. A life in prison was not the life she was expecting to live.

Jessica appeared on the large screen from the newsroom.

"Jessica, we can hear cheering out there! Tell us about the sentencing," John said.

"As many people witnessed on the screens out here and wherever they are around Scotland, it has been a united celebration. Not a normal celebration like the Rangers winning the cup, but Agnes Aird, now prisoner, was found guilty of all seventy-five counts of murder and sentenced to life in prison, John," Jessica stated.

Outside the courthouse, Jessica McGowen interviewed locals about the guilty verdict. Standing next to her was an older gentleman that was affected by the deaths in Beith.

"Sir, how does this guilty verdict resonate with you?" Jessica asked.

The gentleman was notably holding back tears, and he wiped his eyes, and said, "It's about time. My wife was just sitting on our back porch at night. You would think that it was safe, and then shadow took her. Took her! With this verdict, Agnes stays away from Beith, and for that, I'm happy."

"Thank you for sharing that with us," she replied. The camera scanned the area around Jessica, and the group from Beith that had showed up with signs were all cheering.

"So people in Beith are finally at peace?" John asked.

"Excellent question, John. I have it on good authority that there is more going on in Beith and…" Jessica started. "As a matter of fact, there is the councillor of Beith now. Let's talk with him," Jessica said as she moved towards Councillor MacDannels. "Councillor MacDannels, what was your reaction to the verdict and sentencing today?"

He knew he had to answer in a respectable way so as to not make this personal. "Putting it mildly, Beith had succumbed to many misfortunes in the past decades, and many people are quite elated over the current news," he replied.

"Also, I have it on good authority that even though Agnes Aird is out of the picture, Beith is still under a curse. Care to elaborate on that, please?" Jessica asked.

Councillor MacDannels knew that word about the dead would eventually be revealed and that he would have to answer about current developments surrounding Beith.

"As a matter of fact, Jessica, I promised a proper announcement to the citizens of Beith. If you could meet me at my office in an hour, you can have a front-row seat," he said. He forced a shoddy smile, but knowing someone had told her something, he was certain she would not back down until she got her story.

"Well, looks like we are going to Beith for a big announcement that we are hearing first hand! Back to you, John," Jessica said. She looked at Councillor MacDannels, and as she and her cameraman headed towards their news van, she had a cheeky grin, as though this story would bring her another news commendation.

"Jessica McGowen, reporting from Beith inside Councillor MacDannels's office. I talked with him briefly, and he's going to give an account of some of the things manifesting here. I will say, some of what you will hear is disturbing. However, we ask people not to panic," Jessica stated. She and her cameraman sat in a chair adjacent and to the left of Councillor MacDannels's desk and waited for him to go live. A metallic click unlocked the cameras from the ceiling, and they came down like the motion of a robotic arm, facing him. Councillor MacDannels entered the room and took a deep breath before giving his statement.

"Citizens of Scotland. Today Beith revels the conviction of Agnes Aird. For those that did not see the report, she was found guilty of seventy-five counts of murder and sentenced to life in prison without the possibility of parole. Although many may be celebrating this conviction, others are still mourning the loss of their loved ones. We can only hope and pray that this can ultimately be put behind us. However, Beith currently faces another challenge. Apparently when the curse was lifted, those taken came back again. Funerals were held on the sacred land of Renfrewshire, and the tombs became like portals for the dead. Yes, you heard that correctly. Currently the dead are being held at our local community centre and away from our residents. There was one incident, but we have not had any others since that time. With that being said, medical staff have been present and officially stated the dead do not pose a threat to the residents. We are currently allowing family members to visit their loved ones, and we have medical staff, preventive medicine, and religious personnel there for those that require their service. We ask that no one come seeking a glimpse of our returned. This is not a circus show, so please give the residents here respect as they mourn, again, seeing their loved ones. We also have people working on how to get the dead back to where they need to be without causing harm. If there are questions, please do not hesitate to contact my office. Thank you," the councillor concluded.

One of the first questions Jessica wanted to ask was whether they should stop by the community centre, but she refrained from asking. She realised the situation was out of her league, and she wouldn't know how to cover this story further. Jessica told the cameraman, "Cut," to end the live viewing.

"You see why I wanted to keep this to ourselves? We don't need people crowding about here for a peepshow. The health part of it is managed, and there are people who are trying their best to resolve this conundrum. I ask that you leave it be for now," he stated. Jessica was a bit taken aback, as a story was a story and needed to be spoken not suppressed. Yet she understood the nature of it.

"Yes, Councillor. For now," Jessica said. She understood, but Jessica was not the type to back down or become soft on reporting just because it was a fragile situation. "Thank you, and I will see you again soon," she said. They shook hands, and out she went. He didn't want to see her again until the dead finally had peace. That time couldn't come soon enough.

Chapter 3

FAMILY REUNION

"I promise, Auntie," he replied.

"Sabrina isn't going to like this and will worry. It's best you text her as well," Irene stated. Her arms were folded, and at times her hand covered her mouth. Her eyes wanted to just let the tears flow like a broken dam, but she didn't want to break down completely in front of him. The family had suffered so much, and the possibility of losing Daniel made Irene sick to her stomach.

"Yes. I promise, Auntie," Daniel replied. They exchanged a long hug as though he was going to be gone for months. She gave him a moderate smile, acknowledging she understood and that everything would be fine. He returned the smile and departed.

Jeremy and Christian were out on the front porch when Daniel pulled up in his 2075 black Barren MaLark. Although it had a fancy name, it was still the standard four-door vehicle with automatic co-driver system, 3D mapping, predictable accident alert system, heated/cooled seating, satellite connection, and vehicle malfunction alert system.

"Goodness! Where did you find this?" Jeremy taunted as Daniel got out of the car.

"Does it hover like the newer models?" Christian asked.

"I found it for a decent amount in Edinburgh. It gets me where I need to go without hovering, so shut up!" Daniel stated. They all laughed. But the laughter quickly went to silence. It was time for Daniel to get the full story for his return. Jeremy explained what they had seen in front of his mother's house and how the councillor had taken them to the old community centre. Daniel was struggling to process the dead returning and possibly seeing his father and sister.

"When can we go see them?" Daniel asked.

"Oddly enough, there are actual visiting hours. However, you might get an exception," Jeremy said.

"Let's do that then," Daniel replied.

The next morning, Jeremy's mother made a huge Scottish breakfast—eggs, potato cakes, mushrooms, tomatoes, beans, sausage, and fresh bread.

"Goodness, Mum! You outdid yerself. Is the king and queen comin' to our house?" Jeremy asked. He shook his head with slight embarrassment because she always went overboard when there was company.

"You know good and well why I went all out!" Margorie said. She gave Daniel a welcoming smile. "Eat as much as you want, and juices are in the fridge. Have it, laddies," she added.

"Thank you, Mrs. Tucker," Daniel said. His eyes widened with amazement.

"You don't have to be so formal here, Daniel. Everyone calls me Mum. That is, of course, if you so choose to," Mrs. Tucker said.

"Right. Mum. Thank you for the breakfast," Daniel said. He understood the gesture, but it still felt a bit uncomfortable considering he hadn't talked to his own mother yet. Daniel thought about visiting her but quickly shot that thought out of his mind.

"You all right, mate?" Jeremy asked.

"Yeah. I was thinking about whether or not I should visit my mum, but it's not a good idea. There are things I'm still sorting out," Daniel stated.

"I understand. You need to do what's best for you. Goodness. Listen to me like I know what I'm talking about," Jeremy said. He wasn't sure what to say to Daniel.

"Jeremy, I'm fine. I promise. Just be like you normally are. Awkward and intense. That is normal for you, so don't get all peculiar on me, OK?" Daniel stated. Both of them laughed and gave each other a manly hug.

"You got it!" Jeremy replied. "We gotta go pick up Christian before we see your dead kin," he added.

"WOW!" Daniel gasped. "Well, at least I can count on you to be yerself like I asked." He laughed.

"Mum! We're heading to the community centre. Be back later!" Jeremy yelled. His mum was back in the bedroom with the door closed. When she heard him, she quickly opened the door and briskly walked towards them. “Mum. You promised not to get all worried or act weird,” Jeremy added.

“I know, and I’m not. Just making sure you don’t need anything before you go,” Mrs. Tucker said. She began to fidget but knew she had to trust her son’s instincts and that he would alert her if something were to happen while at the centre.

“We’re good, Mum. I’ll call when and if anything extraordinary happens,” Jeremy reassured her.

“OK, sounds good,” Mrs. Tucker said. Margorie took in a deep breath and exhaled slowly to try to calm her nerves. She was more worried for Daniel as he would not be prepared for what was to come.

When Jeremy, Daniel, and Christian arrived at the community centre, they were greeted by a man in a protective suit, Councillor MacDannels, and a priest.

“Looks like my mum called in for your appointment,” Jeremy stated.

“What is a priest doing here?” Christian asked.

“Clearly to pray and throw some holy water or something. I’m sure he’s here to ease the pain of the families,” Daniel suggested.

The councillor was motioning the lads over.

“Daniel, Margorie told me you were back visiting and wanted to see your loved ones. Allow me to introduce to you Father MacArthur.” Father MacArthur greeted Daniel with a smile and a gentle nod. “Father MacArthur comes to us from Glasgow from Saint Agatha’s and is comforting families while trying to determine what and why this delicate situation has occurred," Councillor MacDannels stated.

"Please, call me Father Mac. Many young parishioners call me that," the priest stated. He shook hands with both Jeremy and Christian as well.

"So what do you think happened, Father Mac?" Daniel asked.

"This is not an easy answer. Here is what I believe happened. When this demon, which was in a form of a shadow, took its victims, they were still alive. They remained alive in the netherworld. When the family members conducted funerals on all consecrated land, that provided a portal, for a lack of a better term, by which the dead returned. Unfortunately it is just their bodies and not their true spirit that remains," Father Mac tried to explain.

"So if they got their own spirit back, then they could come back as them again?" Daniel asked enthusiastically. Father Mac looked at Daniel and placed his hand on Daniel's shoulder as though to brace Daniel for the disappointment.

"I am speaking with other fellow priests throughout the United Kingdom. However, biblically speaking, God can give life to the dead. What we are seeing in this building is not something of God. Therefore, in order for their spirits to be set free, they must return from whence they came," he said.

Daniel looked at Father Mac in shock. Then Christian said simply, before Daniel could say a word, "They have to actually die before their spirit can be released."

"That is correct," Father Mac said. He released his hand from Daniel's shoulder and watched as Daniel's eyes became swollen with tears. Daniel wasn't sure what he followed, God or Druidism. He had only recently started going back to church since his auntie was a believer. Yet Daniel couldn't blame his mother for this one anymore. The dead had come back, and their spirits remained in the netherworld. This was more sinister than some blood pact made years ago.

"How can God allow this to happen, Father?" Daniel said. There was anger in his voice but only towards the situation.

"My son. The devil took over the earth the moment Adam and Eve sinned against God. Therefore, we are all sinners, but that doesn't mean God is far away. He is with you as long as you go to Him. Repent, pray, forgive, and love," Father Mac said. He stood at 160 centimetres and had a medium build for an older gentleman. He didn't seem frail like most elderly people. He had white hair that only grew on the sides and the top back of his head. His voice was gentle and calming, yet he spoke the truth with compassion and showed empathy and kindness.

There was silence. The priest waited patiently for any of the lads to speak. Each of them knew it was a lot to take in, yet Jeremy, Christian, and especially Daniel were used to the magical unknown. Daniel looked at Christian, then Jeremy. Jeremy just closed his eyes and shook his head.

"Oi! Daniel's tenacity is going to be the death of me. No pun," Jeremy stated.

“We have to talk to Latrice and find out what we can do, if anything, to get their spirits back from the netherworld,” Daniel persisted. Although he was adamant about seeing Latrice, he had to see first his father and sister. “Thank you, Father, for your assistance,” Daniel said.

“My pleasure. If you need to talk further about anything, here is my card. Call me day or night,” Father Mac said.

Daniel, Christian, and Jeremy nodded to Father Mac, appreciating him, then walked over to the man with the protective suits. Both Jeremy and Christian were ready to join Daniel, but Daniel looked at the both of them and said, “I need to do this alone.”

“No worries, mate. We will be here when you’re finished in there,” Jeremy said.

Daniel donned the protective suit and turned to face Jeremy and Christian and gave them two thumbs up. Daniel walked through the dimly lit foyer, which felt like a kilometre-long walk but was only a few metres. There was a second set of iron doors that led to the dead. Just placing his hand over the wrought-iron handles made his heart palpitate faster. He took a deep breath and told himself, *Cannae turn back now*. As he walked through the doors, he was greeted by two men in protective suits and exchanged a nod as the men motioned Daniel to the first rectangular table. Daniel gave a smile of gratitude in return. Daniel had to wait until he was noticed by his family first, because to approach them could startle them and cause the dead to lash out, as one woman had found out coming to visit her sister. The woman had slowly walked over and touched her sister's shoulder. Before the woman could say anything, the dead sister looked up at her, growled, displayed her sharp teeth, and bit off part of her tricep. Once her cannibal needs were fulfilled, she sat back down as though nothing had happened. Needless to say, the woman required reconstructive surgery, but she was healing well. The blood that couldn't be removed left a reminder of the incident stained upon the brittle stone flooring.

Daniel looked around and noticed that some of the dead were talking coherently. Not fully, but it gave Daniel hope to have that communication with his father and Anna. As he looked to the left, he saw a long glass wall separated him and a recently landscaped enclosed botanical garden. The glass door led to a miniature paradise for the dead. Daniel walked out and looked up at the glass dome ceiling, which looked like crystals. Looking straight on, he saw an array of plants, fir and elm trees, and flowers covering the ground, with each plant having its own descriptive plaque giving the common name, Latin name, and place of origin. There was a pond and a small, red-brick bridge that romantically spanned over the wee stream, which ran through the garden. The mystical landscape of brilliant purples, blues, yellows, and reds gave a cheery notion that even in the gloomiest of times, better days could and would come. It was more than just a biodome; its beauty took them from reality for a while. Daniel scanned every corner of the area for Anna and his father but found nothing. When he looked straight towards a narrow hallway, some figures appeared. His eyes widened. It was Anna and Dad. His heart fluttered, and his body flushed with emotion. Seeing his father again brought tears to his eyes. He wanted to leap out of the chair and hug him, but he knew he had to be patient. As they moved closer, Daniel quietly said, "Dad?"

Thomas looked in Daniel's direction and staggered over to the table. Anna followed close behind. He hugged Daniel, and they all sat down.

"Daniel. It is so good to see you. Let me tell you what is happening. First, Anna comes and goes remembering things, so I need to get to the point before Anna feels like she needs to leave. While we were in the netherworld, Anna was tortured, as you can clearly see. I was not, and I did my best to keep those that were sacrificed by the shadow calm as much as possible," Thomas explained.

"Why was Anna tortured so much?" Daniel asked. He went to reach for Anna's hand, but she pulled away.

"Anna. It's Daniel," Thomas said while looking at her. Daniel took off the protective headgear to prove it was him. The guards came up to the table, but Daniel gently placed the gear on the table, pushed it aside, and motioned to the guards that he would be OK. He waited for Anna's reaction. She was staring down at the table. Then Thomas said again in a tender voice, "Anna. Look, sweetheart. It's Daniel."

She slowly looked up and saw him. Her black eyes quickly became her natural blue. Anna got up from her chair and shuffled towards Daniel. Daniel stood up, and they both embraced. The hug didn't last long, but to hold his sister gave him the closure he needed since he hadn't been at the jubilee when she was taken. Before Thomas could answer Daniel's question, Anna sat down and began to speak.

"I'm not sure how long I have before I go back into my darkness," Anna began. She sounded like herself but very lethargic. Her speech as slow and quiet, almost a whisper. Then she continued. "All I know is that spirits from above were trying to protect me while the demons whipped me. They are after something or someone, but I'm not sure what. One demon said, 'We will find her eventually.'"

"Did they say who?" Daniel asked.

"No," Anna replied.

Daniel thought to himself, *That's odd considering if they wanted Mum, they had every opportunity to take her.* Daniel looked at his father with hope.

"Dad, I talked to the priest. Father Mac. Do you know that your body is here, but your spirit is in the netherworld?"

"If that is the case, then we must be killed in order to be at peace. I see this place as a façade and the demons returning at any moment," Thomas said.

"Dad! There must be another way!" Daniel exclaimed. His heart sank. The pain of losing his family again ripped a hole in his heart.

"Son, I love you, but we do not belong here. We were brought back because the curse was lifted, but we also felt the desire to kill your mother. Reasons I'm sure I don't have to explain," Thomas said.

"You, Anna, and some of the dead I have seen seem to be lucid the longer you're here!" Daniel exclaimed. Thomas could hear the hope in Daniel's voice, but even Thomas knew what had to be done.

"Is it OK if I come back to see you?" Daniel asked.

"Of course! I think the councillor is planning a huge Christmas gathering for families with us as well. Look into that," Thomas replied.

"You think your dead friends will be up to it?" Daniel asked. He had to lighten the mood with some sarcasm. Thomas gave him a cheeky grin in return, and retorted, "I sure hope so."

Both Thomas and Daniel smiled as they shared a father-son moment like old times. It eased the pain for Daniel a bit. However, when he glanced over to Anna, he saw her eyes had returned to full black. The pain inflicted by the demons was in the form of bruises on her arms and face, along with open wounds from razor slashings on her neck and arms. The eyes were an indication of the hate she had for her mother and the emptiness from within. It was difficult to see her this way.

"I love you, Anna," Daniel said softly. Anna glanced over and smiled. Even through the hate she was able to give Daniel that. She stood up and shuffled along the stone floor.

"I better stay with her. Also, if you talk with Sabrina, let her know I love her," Thomas said. He and Daniel stood up and exchanged a hug.

"I will," Daniel replied. Daniel stood as he watched them go back down the narrow hallway. He returned the protective gear and headed into the brisk, cold air to find his mates.

Jeremy and Christian were standing by a vendor selling tea, coffee, hot chocolate, and a variety of biscuits and sandwiches. Daniel ordered a coffee and a cranberry scone.

"So?" Jeremy asked, staring at him in anticipation.

"I'll tell ye on the way to your house," Daniel answered.

"Well, there's a group of people waiting to see you. You can give us the detail then," Jeremy said. He smiled as he took a sip of his hot chocolate. Daniel rolled his eyes and grinned.

As they pulled up to the driveway, Jeremy's front door opened and out ran Judy, Brandon, Latrice, and William. Judy was jumping up and down with excitement.

"I see Judy hasn't changed," Daniel said. Jeremy, Christian, and Daniel laughed.

"Come on, mate," Jeremy said.

They walked up to the house. Daniel was greeted with hugs, cheers, and the normal cheeky jabs.

"See! I told you he couldn't live without us!" Brandon said.

"Don't get all sappy on me, ye sook!" Daniel laughed.

"You know me. I cannae help myself!" Brandon replied.

Daniel glanced over at Judy and gave a slight smirk.

"You're about to jump out of yer skin! Give me a hug already!" Daniel laughed. Judy had no problem obliging the request. She gave him the biggest hug to where he almost couldn't breathe.

They all conjured inside and served themselves the grand food spread of roast beef, beans, salad, tatties, and bread. Mrs. Tucker had outdone herself yet again. As each one grabbed their plate, they sat down and were fixated on Daniel.

"I'm not sure what I saw or heard. Like I saw my father and Anna, but it wasn't them. They weren't whole. My dad is like the lead of the dead and explained that they must die. They are there because the curse was lifted, and since they returned, the other purpose is to kill my mum. Yet their actual spirits remain in the netherworld. That I can't comprehend, so that's for you, Latrice, to help us figure out," Daniel explained.

Latrice nodded. Then he continued. "Anna. None of you are ready for this," Daniel stated. Judy moved to the edge of her seat, while William moved forward to the edge of the couch. William was anticipating the horror Anna had experienced in the netherworld.

"Yeah, so, Anna is definitely not Anna. She said spirits were trying to protect her while demons tortured her. That was evident by the bruises and open wounds on her body," Daniel said. Tears from Judy's eyes trickled down her cheeks, Latrice shook her head with her arms folded in anger, and William had his head down, shedding quiet tears. Christian patted William's back, trying to comfort him.

"One thing Anna said that was peculiar was a demon said, 'We will find her eventually.'"

Latrice looked a bit confused and thought for a moment, then blurted out, "Is Sabrina a witch?"

"No!" Daniel exclaimed. "Auntie wouldn't allow that nonsense in her house. No offence, Latrice," Daniel said.

"None taken," Latrice replied. Then she asked more questions. "Thinking out loud here. Your mum has no power; your auntie is not a Druid nor a witch. Do you have grandparents or other family members who were either witches or Druids?"

"My grandparents passed on and were Druids, and I'm not aware of any cousins," Daniel replied.

"Hmm. I have been out of touch with my witchy ways, but I'm going to research this further," Latrice said.

"Thanks. I appreciate it," Daniel said.

"I just feel the curse may be trying to lure its way back," Latrice said. We need to go back and talk with them further. How is it that we missed something? We destroyed the altar; the curse was lifted; the stones were buried."

"Maybe we'll find some help from our friends from Ireland," Judy said. She looked at Latrice furtively.

"You have friends from Ireland?" Daniel asked.

"It's Druid stuff. We gotta do what we can to figure this out," Latrice said. Latrice quickly looked back at Judy to imply there was something more. "Anyway, I'm going to head home and try to find something on this. There has to be a tome or something we need," she concluded.

"Stop! Just stop! It's Friday! Let's go do something fun. It's early yet. Let's go to Game Hut, to the movies and eat dinner. What say all of you?" Judy asked. It was more like a demand, and they all knew it. She wouldn't back down unless someone had a perfectly good excuse, which no one did. She was waiting for their answers.

"You're not going to take no for an answer, are ye?" Brandon asked.

"Nope!" Judy replied. She stood with her arms folded, tapping her foot.

"Best ovate ever and the biggest pain in the arse. Let's go everyone!" Latrice stated. Judy jumped excitedly, and they all left.

"Hey, Auntie, is it OK if we have haggis and tatties tonight? Rebecca never had haggis before," Sabrina asked.

"Never had haggis? Poor child. Is she Welsh?" Auntie Irene asked. Sabrina chuckled.

"No, but she's never had proper haggis before, so I thought it would be nice," Sabrina said.

"That is a very beautiful gesture, love, but I don't have all the ingredients for it. However, next month when we celebrate Burns Night, you can have her over. Then it will be proper haggis!" Irene stated.

"OK, can we have Scotch pies instead, please?" Sabrina asked.

"Sure," Irene replied.

"Thanks, Auntie!" Sabrina said. She sat on the couch and waited for her best friend to arrive. Sabrina took her auntie's advice and thought it was time to share her thoughts on Beith. A few moments later, Rebecca arrived.

"Hey!" Sabrina said.

"Hey. Hey, Ms. Irene," Rebecca said. Sabrina shut the front door.

"We're having Scotch pie tonight," Sabrina said.

"Cool. I love Scotch pie. Anyway, we really haven't spoken together much, so I was shocked when you asked me over," Rebecca stated.

"I know, and that's my fault. Just when people started talking about Beith, I would just clam up. I was sick and tired of being teased about my mum," Sabrina confessed. "Let's go to my room and talk some more. There is so much going on!"

"I'll let ye know when dinner is ready," Irene said. She smiled. She knew the girls were already gone to Sabrina's room, and they didn't hear her.

"So if you hide things from me like that again, I'll be totally ragin'!" Rebecca exclaimed.

"OK, OK!" Sabrina retorted.

"Give me details on why you get upset about Beith. Like everything!" Rebecca said. They were both lying on the carpet, facing each other. "By the way, your room is a bit creepy. I mean, I understand the love for Jesus, but crosses everywhere is just a bit much, don't you think?" Rebecca stated.

"Yeah, kinda. That's another story," Sabrina said. She was reluctant to tell her auntie's childhood story.

"You asked me over to talk…get chattin'!" Rebecca stated. They both laughed.

"So when my auntie and mum moved to Beith, my mum would secretly read from a forbidden Druid book. Whatever she was reading brought entities from beyond, and well, crosses started turning upside down," Sabrina stated.

"Oh, hell no, bestie. If your room starts doing that mess, I'm out!" Rebecca said. She continued. "Tell me about Beith."

"Honestly, I was angry with Anna for opening the door and allowing the shadow to take our dad. We all knew the rules to stay inside at night, but she had to open the door to look at something and got Dad killed. I wasn't happy when she was taken also when everyone was at the jubilee, but she also deserved that. In my eyes anyway," Sabrina said.

"Dang! That's harsh, but I understand where you are coming from. How did this shadow thing get to Beith? What's the deal with the altar?" Rebecca asked.

"My understanding is this: My mum, with the help of her auntie, who at one time was the second minister, did some sort of blood pact, and if my mum read from the book, she would be a great high priestess someday. That's all she ever wanted. Anyway, she found the missing altar and never told anyone. It was there she worshipped the shadow. She sacrificed the townspeople so she could have powers. That part I didn't know until Daniel came to live here. Needless to say she never had powers and had to fake Druid rituals or whatever the Druids do in their circle," Sabrina said. She was so worried her friend would run out the door and wouldn't speak to her again that her eyes filled with dreadful tears. Rebecca saw her face and put her hand on her wrist.

"You know you're my bestie, right? I'm not going anywhere, and I know you think with all this stuff people are just going to tease you, but I'm not going to do that. Pinkie promise," Rebecca said. She held out her pinkie, and they both locked fingers. Sabrina smiled.

"Besides. All this whack stuff is awesome. Nothing is boring about you. That's for sure!" Rebecca stated.

"Thanks. I think," Sabrina retorted, then laughed.

Irene could hear them laughing, and she was happy for Sabrina.

Rebecca got up and started looking around the room. She shrilled quietly over all the crosses, although some were beautifully hand carved made of birch wood, or Celtic crosses made of wrought iron. Three embellished each wall. Then she looked at the shelf next to her bed.

"I see you still like to read. Have any new books?" Rebecca asked.

"I do, but you can't tell anyone!" Sabrina stated.

"Oh no. You turned to the dark side. You're looking at porn," Rebecca said jokingly.

"Yuck. Seriously?" Sabrina stated.

"And why are some of book covers wrapped in paper?" Rebecca asked.

"I'm still grossed out about the porn thing. Anyway, I wrap them up because it looks like they're schoolbooks. All the books that come into the house have to be seen; basically, the reason is the story I told you earlier," Sabrina answered.

"Holy crap. This book is huge. No way is this a math book," Rebecca said. She opened the book, but Sabrina stopped her.

"Not that one!" Sabrina exclaimed.

"Whoa! What is this? Ms. Irene would rage if she saw this in your room!" Rebecca exclaimed.

"I know. I have been reading up on Druid stuff since my birthday last year. At the time, I figured it would fine to read up and learn chants like my mum did," Sabrina said. The mysterious book was full of incantations and rituals, symbols, and lists of objects needed to prepare the incantations. Items such as ward stones, crystals, and certain rare gems. Its binding and back and front covers were made of hardened white leather, decorated with raised gold. The cover had a woman with long hair holding a pair of stag antlers.

"This is odd. It looks like it's for both Druid and witch. Is there such a person?" Rebecca asked.

"Not that I'm aware of," Sabrina stated.

"So are you believing in this stuff?" Rebecca asked. She looked at Sabrina with concern.

"Not sure what I believe in right now. Speaking of which, Daniel went to Beith to talk to our dad and Anna. I'm not sure if I want to visit them. Cannae be mad at a dead person. I kinda forgave Anna for getting Dad killed but am not really sure how I would feel if I saw her," Sabrina said.

"Lassies, wash up for dinner please!" Irene said.

"Like I asked, please don't tell anyone," Sabrina said.

"No one would believe me if I did, but no, I won't say anything. Pinkie promise," Rebecca said. They locked pinkie fingers and smiled.

Chapter 4

ANNA'S STORY

"Are you ready for your appointment?" Margorie asked.

"Definity yes!" Latrice replied as she happily spread marmalade over her toast.

"What are you so happy about?" Daniel snarled.

Before she took a bite of her toast, Latrice looked at Daniel, and exclaimed, "We are about to break this case wide open, and if my witchy findings are correct, your mother wasn't the only one trying to 'protect' Anna. Agnes was simply a conduit for the shadow's desire for souls."

"What are you talking about?" Daniel asked.

"What I'm saying is there may be someone that we are unaware of also trying to protect Anna, but hopefully after today we will have more answers to prove that theory," Latrice stated.

"That's what we don't need. More people involved. It's too dangerous!" Daniel exclaimed.

"Oh. I completely concur with that statement!" Latrice stated.

"Well, let's get down there and see what we can find out." Daniel sighed.

Daniel and Latrice went into the community centre, and Daniel waited anxiously for his father and sister to appear. Latrice was there strictly for business. Dead or not, she wasn't wasting time and allowing any demons to take over Beith again. When they came down the short, dimly lit hallway, Anna saw Daniel immediately and walked briskly towards him. His father staggered behind her with a beaming smile. Daniel, with a huge smile, eyes widened, opened his arms to her, and they embraced. It was like old times. The fun-loving Anna was back. And although the dead seemed zoetic and accustomed to their surroundings, he had to remain focused because time was limited. It was guaranteed they would all have to die, but no one knew when. In the meantime, Daniel and the people visiting their families here were blessed just for the time they did have.

Anna looked over at Latrice and asked, "Who is this?"

Daniel gave a confused look at Anna, but replied, "This is Latrice. Don't you remember?"

"I remember." Thomas graciously put his arm around Anna and looked at her. "It's OK, Anna. You can trust her," Thomas stated.

Anna looked at Latrice, then looked at Daniel, then nonchalantly said, "OK."

They all sat down at the round corner table, situating themselves in their chairs. Thomas motioned to Anna that it was time to tell her story. Anna gently grabbed Daniel's hand. She was scared, but in her own mind, she knew people had to know what happened.

"I do remember that we were at the jubilee, and I was with friends but not sure who anymore," Anna started.

"That is perfectly fine. Please tell us what happened," Daniel said. His voice was soft and caring like a big brother to his little sister. Anna grinned briefly, then continued.

"The moment I was taken, it went black, like we were flying through a dark mass before arriving at a purple inferno, which led us to what seemed like hell. We arrived on this large, round burning platform where I saw Dad and the others that were taken before me. One by one their arms were chained above their heads as they sat on the burning platform bottom. The shadow left, and I stood there. They saw me and begged me to free them, but there was no way for me to do that. I walked over to the edge of the platform where there was an opening, as though part of the wall was removed. I looked up. It was as though burning bodies were trying to escape up a mountain. When I looked down, you could tell the difference between fire lakes and land masses. Some lakes were black with low flames. Some lakes were black and had some burning bodies in them. The land masses were filled with demons and wolves torturing the burning bodies, and the screaming and moaning never subsided. I was just there maybe five minutes, and it already felt like eternity. Just then the outline of the rune on my arm burned off. Whatever protection I had wasn't there anymore." Anna paused. Daniel caressed her hand a bit.

Latrice thought to herself, *Not sure my level of witchcraft can contend with this.*

"When you're ready, please continue. I'm here for you, Anna," Daniel said. Anna nodded.

"After the rune burned away, a demon appeared who looked like Xerxes in his golden garb. He had a high golden crown that resembled the crown of the ancient Egyptian Nefertari. It also had six emeralds embedded with small pearls hanging from the top of the crown. He also had six red eyes and six fingers on each hand. The demon clamped my arm to ensure I couldn't escape. As if I had somewhere I could escape to. We went through another purple portal that led to the dark king. This large platform could look out to all his dominion. The walls were drapes made of possibly a black silklike material. Eighteen steps led to his throne, and each step was made of gold. Two tall golden vases were used for light. One stood on each side of his throne, and about ten oil laps surrounded the platform or room. There was a woman there, which I presume was the dark king's daughter, with short, curly black hair, full black eyes, a snake's tongue that danced out of her mouth every time she looked at me, and a long tail that resembled a whip. The dark king had an onyx crown with five points, and in the front was an inverted pentagram. He stood over two hundred centimetres and was beyond muscular, which was an understatement, and he had hooves for feet. The dark king looked at his daughter as he saw she was full of death's desire. He smiled deviously, and then suddenly the walls covered with drapes separated, showing the other platform where I was before. The opening of that platform became larger, and four purple portals appeared. Out from those came two very large demons and two wolves, which randomly attacked many of the dead you see walking around here. Every torn flesh, scar, and dismemberment came from them." Anna cried.

"I think that's enough for one day," Thomas said. He looked at both Daniel and Latrice, and as they started to get up from their chairs, Anna stopped them.

"No, there's just a little more. You must hear it before I go back into my darkness," Anna said. She wiped her eyes and continued. "I screamed, 'God please! No!' And the demon still with his death grip on me said, 'God can't hear you here, child.' Then I heard the daughter say, 'The torment pleases me, Father. Thank you.' Her tongue lashing back and forth like she was in some sadistic pleasure moment. Then the demon said to me, 'All this can stop if you just produce your mother.' Then I replied, 'The shadow took me from the jubilee. That was the last time I saw her!' Then some bouncy mini fiery imp with ram horns kept saying, 'Secrets, secrets, secrets.' It was that moment I vanished and found myself covered in dirt in our cemetery," Anna said.

Anna was exhausted. Latrice had many questions but would sort that out later. Thomas delicately took Anna by the hand and motioned for her to go. He looked at Daniel, and said, "It's best if you sought out *your* mother."

Daniel didn't like the way that sounded. This was a level of hate that was beyond Daniel's feelings for his mother. He didn't want to show his disdain, but his thoughts went wild trying to decipher everything. Daniel and Latrice watched as they walked back down the hallway. Daniel continued to stare, and a few moments later, Latrice slapped him.

"Come on with ye. We have lots to discuss!" Latrice said. Daniel came back to the present mentally and gave a nod, and they headed towards her car.

"I think it would be good to get the group together to talk. I never heard of what Anna described, and for her to be that vivid with her description questions her timeline," Latrice said.

"I texted Jeremy, and he'll have everyone there," Daniel said.

"Perfect!" Latrice said.

They approached Jeremy's house. Jeremy was waiting by the window, and by the time Daniel and Latrice reached the porch, Jeremy opened the door.

"Well, everyone is here as ordered, Sir Daniel," Jeremy said.

"Ha. Ha. Very funny. Blame her. Latrice is the one that wanted to call a meeting to order!" Daniel replied. Some quick laughter but then Latrice didn't waste time telling the group what Anna had said.

"Some of that doesn't make sense. The jubilee was months ago. It sounds like the time while in the netherworld was a day for her but months for us," William said.

"Yep," Latrice replied.

"Well, it also sounds like your mum has more secrets. No offence, Daniel," Brandon said. Judy sat next to

Brandon and put her hand over her face. She didn't want to see Daniel's reaction to that.

"None taken," Daniel said. He looked at Judy. "I promise it's OK, Judy."

Judy gave a sigh of relief with a slight grin.

"Yes. Do talk to your mother, Daniel. I found it interesting that your father specified, *your* mother. The demons had ample time to take your mum but didn't. Why?" Latrice asked.

"Can we really rely on Anna's description of things? Meaning what those demons said? Some imp? The devil is a liar! I'm not saying that to be mean, but maybe they said those things to lead her astray and instil fear," Christian said.

"Or they knew the altar would be found and wanted to give her that information to cause strife as they return from the netherworld," Latrice quickly replied. "Or better yet, notice how Thomas and Anna are more vocal than the others. If the netherworld has their spirits, what is not to say they have control of them to find Anna's mother?"

"Well, we have to think of something. Who else in the community can help us?" Judy asked.

"Since when have we become Beith's demon slayers? I'm tired of this crap! And I don't think any of us have healed from the recent events. I know it was a few months ago but still," William yelled. He was not happy about another possible adventure to figure out what demons might be looking for whom and was not interested in any more secrets.

"I totally understand, William. I don't like it any more than you do. However, this is for Anna. This is for your sister." He looked at Brandon. "This is for all the people that lost loved ones due my selfish mum. If I have to figure all this out on my own, I will! Don't you think I'm tired of this shite? This isn't normal. I was fine in Edinburgh. I didn't have to come back here, but I did. So do what you want, but if you can't do it to save Beith, then do it to save our loved ones and find a way to give them rest!" Daniel declared.

"What do you propose then?" Christian asked.

"Well, first things first. Getting back to answering Judy's question, I say that for those that want to help, we spread out and get clues from different people. Maybe Judy and Latrice talk to their Irish Druid friends and see if they know something. I'll go see my mum and bring Christian with me, and then Jeremy, William, and Brandon can go see Father Mac," Daniel directed.

"Jeremy can go with you. I'll go see Father Mac since my family goes to that church anyway," Christian suggested.

"OK, that's great! Anyone else have any ideas?" Daniel asked.

Many just shook their heads no, but William just sat there. Everyone shifted their eyes to William, but he was hesitant to say anything.

"Say it, mate," Daniel said.

"I'm sorry. I just can't get involved, and I can't be arsed with this anymore," William stated. His demeanour was quiet and reserved. William looked around the room and saw the disappointed expressions on everyone's faces. He felt judged, like his decision was wrong even though he felt right. The odd man out.

"I get it, mate, but if Judy was part of the dead, and there was a way to help her, I would do anything," Brandon said. He held Judy's hand tighter, and his eyes began to water. Brandon just shook his head slightly back and forth indicating his disappointment in William.

William stood up from where he was sitting, and yelled, "That is not Anna in the community centre! It's her body but not her! I had to let her go once, and I don't think I can let her go a second time! Do you understand that?" He was emotional and full of tears.

"Sorry, mate. I do understand," Brandon said. He approached William and gave him a hug. When he did, William let the rivers flow. It was evident that William was the one who hadn't yet healed. Everyone else stood up and huddled around William to create a big make-shift hug.

"What shall we do now, Father? I know you have a brilliant plan!" Nixia said. Her eyes widened in suspense of the dark king's next words.

"All of this could have been avoided had the first demon done what he was supposed to. Is it too much to ask to bring souls to me to better my army? Instead, I get disobedience!"

With a wave of his hand, the purple velvet curtains opened, and he looked out to his dominion. He saw the despair and those wailing out, and although it pleased him, he was still upset. The dark king took his anger out on an area near a cliff and from his hand sent a ball of fire to burn them, eliminating their souls forever.

The dark king turned around and faced the open space near the stairs that led to his throne and called upon another demon—Ambrasey.

Ambrasey appeared and knelt before the dark king. This was the same demon that had taken over the mission of the dead in hopes to find the warder. The same demon that Anna described.

"I am at your service, my dark king."

"Rise and hear my plan," the dark king said.

Ambrasey rose and looked down at the ground. Looking at the dark king without permission could lead one to the lake of fire forever. The only one that could look at him was his daughter, Nixia. However, even she had to know her place in the kingdom.

"We have to lure the warder out. If we take Anna back, her friends will look for ways to rescue her. In their ventures, they may find her actual mother. Doing so will lure her out, and we can take her as well. That would leave only the warder. For now"—the dark king caressed Ambrasey's face—"you will take Anna and bring her back here. Soon I think we will have a family reunion."

"Bringing the child here will be my absolute pleasure, my dark king," Ambrasey said.

"I know it will. It is why I have tasked you. There is a time and place for everything, so I'm leaving it up to you for the timing. However, make haste with your decision. I don't want those Druid brats and their friends finding anything that could ward off my plan!" the dark king exclaimed.

"As for you, my child, you will find the black book and have it protected. I will send Ambrasey when the time is right to use it again to collect all the souls of Beith. We will start there and take all of Scotland and then the rest of the world!" he said. There was a pause, and he then continued. "I don't think I have to remind you what happens if you fail me. Both of you can be replaced, but I would much rather have my two most trusted demons on this. Now go!"

They both bowed to him and vanished.

Nixia went to her throne room. She was in control of the southern area of the netherworld where she could torture as many souls as she wanted. Or she could have the demons torture souls for her as she watched with delight. Her room was the one place that her thoughts were safe and where she could say or do anything she desired.

She would do anything for the dark king. Anything! However, the moment sarcastically he mentioned a family reunion, it reminded Nixia of when the dark king and her mother, Lilian, had roamed the earth. They would attend operas, symphonies, and plays for their evening pastime, dressed in purple or blue velvet. It was her mother's favourite. During the day, they gratified each other and tortured those whom they had lured into their den.

One night, Father brought in a child to torture, a young girl in her teens taken from the streets of Glasgow. Father thought it would be wise to teach her a lesson on what her sin would give her. Lilian begged the dark king to let her go and tried to convince him to find others, but he refused. She continued, and because of her disrespect and denial of what he wanted, she was banished from him. She now sat in a tower on the east side of the kingdom, where Nixia was forbidden to go.

There were many times Nixia was conflicted in her feelings. She was born to hate and be grateful that the dark king had allowed her to live, but she felt other things as well and could not explain it. Love was not an option here, and saying the word could get you punished in the sea of souls, the place where only your head was shown because your body below the sea was burning or being gnawed on by the creatures. Demons could step on you. It just so happened at that moment, Nixia looked out from her room to see demons play hopscotch on their heads. She laughed, and yelled out to them, "Well done!" The demons saw her and bowed, but she told them to continue.

It wasn't long after that she sat on the pentagram on the floor and began to chant. Her time of reminiscing was done, and she had to find the black book. She knew it was hidden somewhere and still believed it was within the house. She couldn't directly ask Laurie because the *enemy* had her and the woman that had repented, Catlin. The last place she knew of the book's location was in Laurie's house. Nixia knew her mother was still there and decided to ensure when she slept, her dreams were full of nightmares. Bloodthirsty nightmares. Nixia even added the images of the torture given to the dead before returning to Beith. Nixia knew if the mother wanted the nightmares to stop, she would have to reveal the book, hence breaking the protection spell.

"Nixia!" the dark king called to her from beyond. She vanished and instantly arrived at her father's chambers.

"Yes, Father. How may I serve you?"

"Your thoughts are not safe, my dear. You do know why your mother is locked away, don't you?" he said. He walked over to her and grabbed her neck and made her look at him. "It is because she was disobedient. You disobey, you are punished. I do believe I give simple rules to follow, do I not?"

"You do, Father," Nixia replied, shivering in fear.

"Then why, in the most minuscule way, would you even think about her?" he asked.

"I'm not sure why I became weak, Father, but it waned when I watched the demons play on the heads in the sea of souls. The torture made me feel much better and brought me back to reality," she replied.

Tightening his grip on her neck, the dark king opened the curtains to the east. Her body was perfect and naked for all the demons and souls to see. This area was known as the Cliffs of Lust, and it was the most repulsive area of the dominion.

The dark king changed Nixia's vision to see her mother as though she were looking through binoculars. The open tower with only four rounded pillars held her mother captive. She couldn't vanish within the netherworld or go to earth to see her operas. She was alone in one area for eternity.

"There! Does that give you incentive, child, not to think about her and not be disobedient to me?" the dark king yelled. He threw her across the floor, and Nixia rubbed her neck and tried to breathe.

"Yes, Father," she muttered, still gasping for air.

"Then I strongly suggest you find the black book and not think about her again, or you may end up just like her," he said, glaring at her.

She vanished before he could grab her again.

A storm was coming. White and grey clouds from the west glided across the sky and showed a motif of designs painted by the wind. It would not be long before the friction in the air would cause bouts of lightning and squalls of rain.

Luckily for the returned, they could watch the aerial wonder from inside the dome.

Councillor MacDannels and some of his committee members were standing at the back of the community centre discussing ways to expand the building without causing destruction to the original structure. He felt that the returned shouldn't be cramped up and should be allowed more space to roam. Many argued that if they had more space, it would cause them to be easily startled and cause damage, while others said it was just too expensive and not worth the trouble. All agreed they hoped the Druids and anyone helping them would develop a plan soon to resolve this situation all together.

"We can discuss this further back at the office," Councillor MacDannels stated. He felt some raindrops splashing on his coat. All agreed.

Although the weather was unpredictable, inside was a typical day. Families would come and spend time with their returned, bringing photo albums in hopes of jarring their memories. Most of the time, the album was the returned staring off into the distance while the family would tell them about their day or try to get them to remember something. The family didn't mind. They were just happy to have them there, even if it was just for a little while.

Thomas and Anna were walking through the halls. Anna said, "Daniel?"

Thomas was shocked a little, and replied, "Yes, Daniel is your brother and was here earlier."

She said again, "Daniel but no Sabrina." Her eyes went black. Thomas immediately rubbed her back, and replied, "Sabrina is at Auntie's house. She is safe."

Her eyes went back to normal, and she smiled. "Sabrina is safe."

Thomas smiled back at her. He thought to himself that it took a lot out of her just to tell her story. It saddened him to see her like this, as though part of her soul had been drained away, but from what she has gone through, it was understandable. He wished that he had been tortured more than Anna, but there was no way to save her in that regard. All he knew was that Agnes was at fault. He had to suppress his thoughts from making himself angry to avoid the others from possibly causing a commotion.

They took another stroll around the centre, and he led her out to the dome. Maybe seeing the rain, the mini waterfall, and the plants would calm her a little more. There were benches recently placed along the river, and Anna had one particular spot where she liked to sit. Just past the door leading to the dome area was one bench that faced east, where she could view everything—the plants, the river, the clouds above. There she felt at ease. Anna would swing her legs from under the bench and smile. It was slight, but Thomas noticed. He took his finger and gently rubbed her cheek and pulled her close to give her a hug. Some of the returned in the dome noticed and instantly sat by the river, gazing into the water with bliss.

Anna looked at the clouds and noticed they had shifted to a different direction. She pointed up to the sky, and said, "Bad clouds!"

Thomas tried to relax her. "It's OK, love. It just means there's a storm coming." He also looked up and noticed the clouds moving north instead of west to east. It had been noted before that when this happened, it would be more than a storm moving through, such as microbursts and other anomalies.

He took her by the hand and helped her stand. She placed her hand on his upper arm as though she was being escorted to a dance. It was getting darker, so the lights that hung along the walls went from dim to full light.

Thomas had a faint memory of Anna when she was younger. On the weekends they would watch a movie or two or sometimes three. There was always something to eat and drink thanks to Agnes thinking someone would starve. When the credits rolled, Thomas would look at the couch and notice Anna was asleep. He would scoop her up and take her to her bed, tuck her in, and give her a kiss on her forehead. He would also make sure her ruby gem night light was turned on. Anna was so proud of it since that was her first electrical item she made with her gems.

This time there was no tucking her in. The dead didn't sleep. They walked aimlessly throughout the centre still waiting for the opportunity to kill Agnes. Little did they know they would never get that opportunity since Agnes had already been tried and sent to prison.

They came around another corner, and Anna looked up and pointed at something. Anna had absolute fear in her eyes.

"Anna! What is it?" Thomas exclaimed. He tried not to be too loud, but her actions caught the attention of some of the returned.

"The golden demon. He's standing right there!" Anna yelled. When she yelled, some of the returned started to growl, thinking it might be Agnes. Thomas looked in the direction she was pointing, but nothing was there. He tried to calm her, but she insisted the golden demon was right in front of her. In a split second, a purple inferno appeared, and then she was gone.

The others stopped growling and shuffled along their way as though nothing happened. There was no way to reach out to anyone because that would scare the townspeople. He had to wait until he saw Daniel-- or *if* he saw Daniel again.

Ambrasey arrived back to the netherworld with Anna with a tight grip on the back of her neck.

"Bring the child to me," the dark king demanded.

The demon threw Anna before the dark king's feet. While she was on the ground, the dark king clutched her face in his hand and sniffed her.

"With your spirit hanging in the balance, I'm amazed at your tenacity. Do you honestly think you will ever make it out of here alive? Don't answer that because the answer is no. It was a rhetorical question, of course. However, your friends will look for you and lure out the people we need. In the meantime, enjoy your stay."

The dark king vanished Anna to a separate pod with a round platform that could hold four people. The floor was made of old bones, and it barely floated above the steaming fire lakes below. Anna was more coherent compared to when she was at the centre. She tried to think who the dark king was after since her mother was out in the open. He could have what he wanted at any moment but refused to take her. None of it made sense to her. She covered her ears for a while to muffle the nearby screams. Some of the dead that were in the fire tried to grab a hold of her pod, but each time they would slip back into the fire. She knew God couldn't hear her, but she prayed none of the demons with their hounds would torture her again.

The dark king then called for Nixia.

"Have you retrieved the black book yet? Let me guess. No. How is it my greatest demon can teleport to right where Anna was and bring her here, but you can't bring me a simple book?"

"Normally, it would be a simple task, Father. However, this book is currently under a cloaking spell, and the spell can't be broken unless it's actually found. If my plan with the mother works, which I'm sure it will, then it will be found very soon. When it is, I'll bring it back here so there's no interference in maintaining your plan," Nixia replied.

"Leave me! And don't come back unless you have the book!" the dark king yelled.

Nixia vanished to her throne room. She knew her thoughts wouldn't be safe, but she was sick and tired of her father's antics. She knew he needed souls for his army, but this had become a peculiar obsession to find a witch and a Druid. There was something he was not telling her. *Why this witch? Why this Druid? Why is Anna so special? All of this because Agnes was disobedient? Because of a pact that was made long ago?* Nixia's mind was flooded with questions but no answers. She recalled what happened to the demon that couldn't provide souls for him. The altar was found, and the demon believed that the human, Agnes, would bring him souls. He relied more on the human than essentially doing the task he was given.

The more she thought about it, the more it made sense to her. It was all about her father winning when others were being tested. It didn't matter how big or small their part was in his play, if someone didn't produce, anyone in his way would suffer.

Chapter 5

THE CONFESSION

Judy took the number out from her purse. She looked at Latrice, and Latrice looked back at Judy hesitantly.

"I hope this works," Judy said. She dialled the array of numbers, and after a few seconds, pulsing rings buzzed at the other end. At least three sets went by, and just when she was about to hang up, an angelic voice was heard.

"Hello," a lady answered. Judy froze.

"Hello. Can you hear me?" the lady said. Her voice became irritated. Latrice stared at the phone and then snatched it from Judy's trembling hands.

"Yes, sorry, is this Siobhan?" Latrice asked. [*Pronounced shh vone*].

"Who wants to know?" the lady asked. The brash tone in her voice indicated she didn't like surprising calls.

"My name is Latrice, high priestess of the grove here in Scotland. Your sister gave me your information," Latrice stated firmly.

A small chuckle reverberated in Latrice's ear.

"My sister? I don't have a sister. Especially in Scotland!" she exclaimed.

Latrice's patience was worn thin at this point. The Irish and Scottish normally did not quarrel, but if this was the woman they needed, then Latrice would have to find a way to convince her to help them.

"Oh, is this you trying not to be in the queen's shadow?" Latrice stated boldly. It was more of a statement, and she wasn't going to keep playing her games. There was a pause. Latrice for sure thought she would hang up. Judy was constantly whispering, "What is she saying?"

"You have my attention. If the queen gave you my number, then it must be important. And yes, my name is Siobhan. You must be from Beith since there is nothing happening in any other part of your country. I take it your town is still under a curse?" Siobhan asked. Her voice insinuated that she knew more. Latrice was shocked. How would another grove know more than them? Yet Latrice had to nonchalantly inquire for an answer.

"What do you mean?" Latrice asked. Her voice was calm as to not give away that there was a problem anywhere, especially in Beith.

"Since I and a few of my grove are heading to Glasgow for holiday in two days' time, it would be best to speak then," Siobhan stated. It was very matter of fact, and Latrice knew there was definitely more to say. Ultimately Beith was nowhere close to freedom.

"Oh, and don't tell *Her Majesty* I'm coming. We haven't spoken in a while, and I don't want her to fuss over me with all that royalty crap!" Siobhan stated. Her tone was laced with sarcasm. It was blatantly clear there was still disdain towards her sister.

"She is actually very nice. I hope your visit will render a prosperous relationship," Latrice started. Latrice had to remember that she was a high priestess now and had to put her own personal intentions aside. "Perhaps we can join our groves and do the Winter Solstice ceremony!" Judy's eyes lit up with delight.

"That's a brilliant idea! I'll call you when we're settled," Siobhan stated. The call ended. Seemed more abrupt and unsettling. Latrice didn't like how this felt at all and wondered if calling upon another grove was a good idea. Judy wouldn't stop tugging on Latrice for all the consequential information.

"Oh my gosh, Judy!" Latrice exclaimed.

"Sorry, just need to know everything!" Judy said excitedly.

"Of course you do. Sorry I snapped, but it seems as though the ladies from the Irish grove will be coming to Glasgow and will contact me when they arrive. Siobhan, as you heard, is willing to do the Winter Solstice with us. What has me worried is that she indicated that Beith is still under a curse. I can't shake that off," Latrice stated. Her persona changed. It was as if dread instantaneously embodied her. It was not often she allowed fear to control her, but she felt as if this was different.

"That's impossible! We destroyed the altar!" Judy exclaimed.

"Well, we will find out in two days what they have to say," Latrice said.

"To be fair, since the dead have returned, I think we all have become aware of the curse possibly returning," Judy stated.

"Wise words. Let's go see how the others are doing," Latrice said. She didn't like the truth being thrown at her, but there was no time to be egocentric. If the grove and Beith were to survive at this point, it had to be due to humility.

Christian and Brandon headed to the cathedral on Parson Street. The building had been standing firm since the early seventeenth century with minor renovations to present day. As they approached, Christian was awestruck by its architecture. Although many cathedrals and buildings represented the Gothic period, it was very likely that James VI, heavily admiring Renaissance art, mathematics, and literature, influenced the last-known building of its kind before implementing the Baroque period. It had been said that he sought refuge there during his reign, a quiet space to process his internal conflicts. Everything about the building was symmetric. Rounded pillars on each side of the rounded archway stood guard leading into the cathedral. Statues of angels graced the pillar top, and stained-glass windows surrounding the main building represented the Stations of the Cross. Towards the back, the building was L-shaped and led to prayer rooms and classrooms and it was also adorned with mirroring rounded archways along with a walkway. The building wasn't the old dreary, grey brick but a welcoming stucco and light-brown stone. The exterior was bedecked with circular and rectangular designs, in which no space was bare. As they entered, there was an enclosed, long, horizontal entry room where one could greet the priest, look at reading material, or observe the service. Past the double glass and wooden doors, their senses were engulfed with mystery and history. The ceilings were high, and in the centre was a hollow dome that displayed twelve saints. The dome was held up by four large white marble pillars. There were also four columns of twelve newly polished wooden pews, where people were seen praying or just admiring the architecture like Christian appeared to be.

Brandon wasn't amused or interested but just wanted to see Father Mac. He became confused when he looked at Christian and saw silent tears. Those tears were tears of joy and confusion. Christian thought to himself, *How are we in Beith living through such despair and yet feel adoration in this holy place?* His emotions overcame him, and he slumped down in the nearest pew as though his body had become weightless.

Brandon sat down beside him in bewilderment, not sure how to comfort his friend. He shook his head in self-defeat, thinking no one outside of Beith would understand the absolute devastation Beith endured. Brandon started to worry about what Father Mac would say to or about them after he heard their stories. It was only a few moments later when Father Mac walked up, holding a box of tissues, and sat in the pew in front of them. He placed his hand on Christian's shoulder to alert him he was there and then interlaced his hands.

"What troubles ye, my son?" Father Mac asked. Christian didn't answer, and Brandon wasn't sure how to respond either. Father Mac looked at Brandon in hopes for a possible answer, but Brandon just shrugged his shoulders. Father Mac was patient. He had learned after being a priest for more than thirty years that you get more information when you wait than when you rush. Bide yer time or the geese will tell it in the autumn, meaning all will be revealed in due course. He handed the tissue box to Brandon, and he jabbed the box at Christian's arm.

"Thanks," Christian said while wiping his face. Then he looked up at Father Mac, and said, "Sorry."

"No need to be sorry," Father Mac replied. He gave a slight smile to reassure Christian of his sincerity.

"It's just that Beith seems to be covered by the curse, but when I walked in here, I felt safe. I know it sounds stupid but—" Christian began to say before Father Mac politely cut him off.

"Not daft at all. God always surrounds us," he said. Christian smiled.

While Christian was gathering his composure, Brandon stated bluntly yet in a loud whisper, "Father, we need help trying to find a way to give the living dead rest!"

"Ah yes. This conversation may be better suited to one of our classrooms. This way, gentlemen," Father Mac said as he led them to one of the classrooms. Christian and Brandon sat on one side of the long rectangular tables and Father Mac sat adjacent to them. Then he began again. "I had spoken to a few other priests about Beith.

Although prayer may help, this deserves the attention of someone higher in the priestly authority. There are only a few, hand-selected ritualists from the pope, and one of them happens to live in Edinburgh."

"Ritualists?" Brandon asked.

"Oh my. That sounds more like witchcraft. The church is involved in witchcraft? This will be very interesting to one of our friends!" Christian exclaimed.

"Let's not jump to misconceptions, laddies. A ritualist in this regard is one that knows about ancient tomes and writings, how they are used, and how to protect the church when such negative activities present themselves. Although many ritualists are religious by nature, some are set aside for researching other types of, shall I say, *practices*," Father Mac stated.

Christian asked frankly, "So your priest friend in Edinburgh knows about Druidism?" The tone was subtle yet abrasive. Brandon immediately picked up on it.

"I guess the bigger question is how long has this priest known about the happenin's in Beith? And better yet, why didn't he or anyone intervene? This has been goin' on for decades, and we are hearing about this so-called 'ritualist' now?!" Brandon yelled. His face was red, and he was remembering when the shadow took his sister. Tears of anger sheathed his face.

Father Mac softly tried to calm them down, but right now, he was more worried about losing their trust.

"I understand your frustrations, and they are valid; however, I'm just the messenger of information. If I were able, I would have helped many years ago. Father

Anthony David, the ritualist, has also known for many years. It was addressed to His Holiness, and he deemed it was not necessary to get involved. I'm quite certain after hearing the latest promulgations, his interests in the matter had been amplified. With that being said, I did find out some information that may be helpful to your Druid friends."

"Please forgive me for yellin' at ye, Father. Yes, anything would be helpful," Brandon felt sheepish for his behaviour.

"My son, God forgives us in our anger. As long as we don't hold tightly on to that emotion, we can be set free. Now as a priest, I don't believe in using books other than the Bible to find answers; however, Father David expressed to me that there is a tome that is used to fight off the darkness. Do you know of such a tome?" Father Mac asked.

"No, but maybe our friend does," Brandon replied.

"Do we know where to find this tome?" Chistian asked.

"Excellent question that cannot be answered. You would think that it would be in the archives in Edinburgh, but apparently that is not the case. It was stolen and last seen here somewhere in Glasgow. That tome needs to be in the archives. If used improperly, it could cause more damage than good. I'm sorry for not having more answers for you, but I was blessed to even get that much out of him. And please don't go to Edinburgh and disturb Father David. I saw it in your faces." Father Mac smirked.

"Can we call on ye if we need help again, Father?" Brandon asked.

"Absolutely!" Father Mac pulled out some cards with his contact information and handed the cards to them. Brandon and Christian expressed their gratitude towards Father Mac.

"Well, if you don't mind, I have to prepare for the next service. Just know you are welcome any time." Father Mac showed them out and gave a small prayer as they continued their journey into the unknown.

"I didn't notice it until now, but I got a text from Latrice sayin' to meet at Jeremy's house," Brandon mentioned.

"I figured. I'm anxious to find out what went on with everyone else," Christian stated.

Daniel and Jeremy walked into the newly renovated Glasgow police station. Looking at the front of the main building, they saw it was three stories, while the left and right wings were only two. The tan-brick building with parts of the frame painted blue, which resembled the Scottish flag, seemed welcoming, until you went inside and approached the desk officer.

"Officer, I'm here to see my mum, Agnes Aird," Daniel said.

"Do you have an appointment?" the officer asked. She looked at Daniel as though he was interrupting her day.

"An appointment? Was not aware I needed one. Please, Officer, we won't be long, but I need vital information from her," Daniel pleaded. The officer rolled her eyes. She lifted the handset from her desk phone and called for another officer on the intercom. Soon after the call, they could hear gated doors opening and clanging back closed. A male officer appeared and looked even more disgruntled than the desk officer.

"Take these lads to see their mum. Thirty minutes should do," the officer stated.

"Follow me and stay close," the male officer said.

Daniel looked at the desk officer, and said, "Thank you." She nodded and was able to muster a slight grin as though to say, "*You're welcome but don't ask for anymore favours.*"

The desk officer buzzed the initial door to the east wing. Daniel and Jeremy didn't say a word and followed the officer as instructed. Once the door shut behind them, the officer became friendly.

"So you're here to see 'Mother Murderer'?" the officer asked.

Daniel and Jeremy looked at each other, and Jeremy's eyes widened as though to exert the connotation, "*Did he really just say that*?" Daniel wasn't sure how to respond.

"Officer, if I may ask, could you please call her prisoner or Mrs. Aird around family? We already know what she has done. And yes, that is who we are here to see," Daniel retorted. His family had been murdered, except for Sabrina, and Daniel's and Sabrina's reputations were already tarnished thanks to their mum.

The officer smirked. "I understand. Sorry about that. She's been on suicide watch since she arrived here, so we cannae send her to prison just yet. Hopefully after your talk that will move things along to get her out of here," the officer stated.

Daniel didn't respond. They reached the middle of the long corridor and turned left towards the centre. The officer used his radio to get the floor officer to open the gate. The gate moved across its rails, like heavy chains being dragged across the floor. Once they walked across the threshold, the gate immediately closed behind them. Jeremy jumped a little when the gate slammed shut. As they walked closer to the centre gate, Daniel felt a chill overcome him. All of a sudden, time seemed to go slower and slower. The inevitable time to see his mum and not knowing what to expect made the hairs on his arms rise. The officer announced on this radio to open the gate, and as they walked through, there was another desk officer, and in front of him was a large room with three square glass pods. Each pod held a prisoner that was on suicide watch. The whole area was a dodecagon, and each side held a prisoner waiting to go to the proper HMP.

Daniel just stood at the desk and found his mum in one of the pods. She was just sitting there. Not readin', not watchin' the telly, just doing nothing. Daniel instantly became flooded with anxiety and wasn't sure if he could talk with her.

"Mate, I know what you're feelin'. I'll be right there with ye. You're going to be OK," Jeremy reassured him.

Daniel seemed to muster some deep breaths and slowly walked towards the pod. One of the officers placed an additional chair in front of the pod. It was then Agnes looked up, and when she saw Daniel, she was so pleased to see him. Tears of joy ran down her pale cheeks, and she stood up to greet him.

"Oh, my dear boy. Daniel. It's wonderful to see you," Agnes gleefully said. Daniel looked at her but couldn't muster a word. Jeremy felt he should step in to get the conversation going since they didn't have much time.

"Ah, hi, Mrs. Aird. Daniel is in a wee bit of shock at the moment, but we do have to ask you some questions without lots of explanation. Are you willing to talk no matter how difficult the question?" Jeremy asked.

Before Agnes could answer, Daniel shook off his anxiety, and spouted out, "Mum, I have talked with Anna and Dad, and Anna mentioned that from her experience, those not of this world are looking for her mother. Dad distinctively said, 'Go talk to *your* mother.' There are things that are goin' on right now that we don't have time to explain, but you, I'm sure, have plenty to say. So spill it, Mum!" Daniel demanded.

The joy Agnes had in her eyes quickly subsided. The conversation exhibited as a chessboard displayed checkmate, and she knew she had to convey any and all secrets. She took a moment to gather her thoughts.

"We were trying to get pregnant, but it just wasn't happening for whatever reason. You were two years old when we brought Anna home, and you loved her so much! It wasn't easy keeping the secret as time went on because I didn't have pregnancy photos of me and Anna," Agnes said.

"What secret?" Daniel asked. He sat up in his chair and glared at Agnes.

"Remember that time you did some lineage project in primary school? I was reminded then to keep the truth about Anna even more a secret. So to keep you from asking to see those photos from when I was pregnant with you, I hid them. Out of sight, out of mind I thought would be best. You see, most of our kin died when I was young except that my great-aunt Deborah had a relationship with a man named Derrick, and they had a daughter Samantha. I believe she became a Druid. She in turn had a boyfriend but never married, and they had a daughter named Julia, who decided not to be a Druid but a witch. Unfortunately she was raped and felt too embarrassed, became incredibly depressed, and decided to seclude herself from others. She bore a daughter…" Agnes became silent.

Daniel yelled, "What is her name!?"

Agnes sighed and looked at Daniel.

"Anna," she said. Then she continued. "So technically Anna is your cousin. I didn't know about this lineage until Julia found me and called me to arrange the adoption,"

By this time, Daniel had his arms folded across his chest, and Jeremy had a tight grip on his chair, shifting his eyes, wondering what Daniel was going to say. He was quiet. Too quiet. Daniel wanted to break the glass that separated him and his mum. He wanted to scream but unequivocally had to keep his composure. He looked at Jeremy and moved his hand from the chair to his lap.

The blood rushed back into Jeremy's hand. Then Daniel broke his silence.

"Where can we find this Julia?" Daniel asked.

"I promised Julia I would keep Anna safe and not reveal Julia's whereabouts," Agnes stated.

"That's funny. Keeping Anna safe. Lotta good that did, right, Mum?" Daniel said. "You have seemed to forget where you are right now, and any *protection* you think you're providing is void. Tell me where to find her!"

"Her name is Julia Shaw. It's been sixteen years, and she may have relocated. Last I knew, she was near Dunino Den," Agnes said. Daniel took one last look at his mum, he rose from his chair, turned around, and started walking towards the desk officer. Jeremy followed suit. Agnes tapped on the glass. "Daniel! Daniel! Please come back to see me. Daniel!"

The officer smacked his fist on the glass to shut her up. Daniel was silent walking back. The loud clang of closing gates didn't faze him. He couldn't decide which was more deceptive: his mother's delusion of power that had led to murder or her hiding the fact that his sister was actually his cousin. They got to Jeremy's car, and Daniel realised he should have listened to Auntie Irene and not come to Beith. It was duly noted that he would see and hear things that would mentally stress him out.

"Take me to my old house, please," Daniel stated.

Jeremy was scared. Daniel was too calm, and wanting to go to his old house meant two things: either he was going to break stuff or he simply wanted to look one last time before moving on. Jeremy bet in his own mind he was going to break stuff.

They arrived, and on the lawn was a For Sale sign. Daniel sighed. He slowly turned the key to unlock the door, and immediately he was flushed with rage. Ghostly images of memories appeared. The time Anna ran through the house with all her rubies. When she slipped on the ice and had a huge bruise on her leg. Watching the telly or playing games. Sharing secrets. He still remembered the time when Anna revealed she loved William. She was only thirteen. It was then that Daniel let out a thunderous yell that shook the house like an earthquake. He ran upstairs and stormed into his parents' room. The oval mirror, the vanity; whatever he thought was hers, he took all his strength and obliterated it. He yelled, "I HATE YOU! I HATE YOU!"

Jeremy thought, *Yep, I knew he was goin' to break stuff.* Jeremy ran upstairs and grabbed Daniel to stop him from destroying the room. Daniel tried to fight him off but couldn't. Then Daniel dropped to his knees, placing his hands over his face, and just cried. Greetin' until his tears ran dry. Jeremy helped him up, and they went back downstairs. Daniel acted as though nothing happened, and said, "I'll have to get help to clear out the personal items, but the rest can be sold."

"Mate. Seriously? Yer aff yer heid just a moment ago and now actin' sane? What the bloody hell!?" Jeremy exclaimed.

"You're right. I'm sorry. I was a complete eejit! But I feel better," Daniel said. He raised his eyebrows and gave a puppy-dog look to Jeremy as though he was asking for forgiveness.

They exchanged a manly hug, and then Jeremy grabbed him by the shoulders, and said, "Don't you ever do that again or I'll punch you in your face!"

"OK. OK!" Daniel said, and both of them laughed. Daniel looking at his phone, "looks like Latrice and Judy are already at your house."

"Always my house." Jeremy rolled his eyes as he stated this sarcastically.

"You really want to come here?" Daniel inquired.

"Noted," Jeremy answered.

Soon they arrived at Jeremy's house, and were greeted by Judy and Latrice.

"We weren't here long," Latrice said.

"Clearly. And my mum has been overbearingly hospitable as usual I see," Jeremy stated. He noticed all the food and drinks across the counter.

"You know I don't mind at all. I like that my house serves as a meeting place. It's fun," Jeremy's mum said, grinning from ear to ear.

"Ah, here comes Brandon and Christian now. Good because there is LOTS to discuss. The emphasis on lots!" Jeremy exclaimed.

"You probably have more than us. Well, for now anyway," Latrice said.

Brandon and Christian came through the door, and Brandon was embraced by Judy. They looked exhausted. Judy instantly became concerned. Brandon whispered that he'd explain in a moment.

"So who wants to go first?" Daniel asked. The question was cheeky in nature.

"Ah, that was an indicator that you should go first," Christian said.

"Correct. So long story short, Anna is my cousin, and we went over to my house, and I tore up some of my mum's stuff. Who's next?" Daniel retorted. Every jaw dropped. Then Jeremy helped fill in the gaps.

"Yeah, so allow me. Daniel is aff his heid at the moment. So we went to the police station where his mum was held in a pod, basically because she's on suicide watch since the trial. She then went into this lineage of how Anna's real mother gave her up because she was raped and became depressed. Apparently it was impeccable timing because Agnes felt like she couldn't give birth or something. And although most of the family were Druids, Julia Shaw, Anna's mum, was a witch. As far as we know, Julia is possibly at Dunino Den."

"Why would a witch hide in ruins of ancient Druidism?" Latrice asked. Then she thought for a moment. "That's actually brilliant. No one would suspect a witch there, and so her identity would be obscured."

Judy exclaimed instantly, "You know what this means, right?" Everyone looked clueless.

"The lineage. Latrice, Anna is just like you. A witch and a Druid. She may not be a practicing witch or Druid, but her bloodline suggests that it's possible that Julia put the protective rune on Anna. We need to find that out. We may find what we need to break the curse once and for all if we unearth who did it!"

"A tome possibly," Christian simply stated.

"What?" Latrice asked. His comment piqued her interest.

"Brandon and I visited Father Mac today, and it appears that much of Scotland, and the Pope, have known about the situation in Beith for decades. However, it didn't seem pressing enough to intervene," Christian said.

"Yeah. Apparently there is a ritualist in Edinburgh that's been keepin' tabs on Beith and the way the Druids have been handlin' the curse. From what I gathered, if what was happening here didn't interfere with the church, then they didn't pursue involving themselves," Brandon clarified.

"Gotta love those arrogant Catholics. Always thinking about themselves!" Latrice stated.

Judy turned to Latrice, and yelled, "Stop it! We mustn't say such things. It is clear that not all Catholics hold the same beliefs, or we wouldn't have received the information from Father Mac. We are—well, most of us--are Druids! We bring peace, not agitate the hate that surrounds us! As a high priestess, I expected better from you. Denounce me as your ovate but I stand firm in my convictions!" It was clear that she was fed up with everything and everyone. Judy, the gang's cheerleader, undoubtedly had to let go of her stress that she had been holding on to. The thought of the curse rearing its head over Beith again put everyone on edge.

"Again, you bring wisdom and truth when necessary. It is I that requests your forgiveness, as my actions call for it," Latrice stated. The shame overwhelmed her. No one had ever seen her like this before. Always headstrong.

Judy didn't say anything but turned to Brandon. "Did Father Mac say anything else?"

"No, not really, other than this tome belongs in the archives or bad things could happen in the wrong hands," Brandon answered.

Judy thought for a moment. "Hmm. If Laurie had the black book, would the tome be a white book? Silly, but the tome must be something opposite of the black book. Good-versus-evil type of thing."

"I think you're on the right track. Maybe something for us to ask Julia when we find her!" Latrice stated. It seemed Latrice had snapped back to her normal, aggressive self.

"What about you guys? Was the luck of the Irish on your side?" Brandon asked.

"Kinda. They are coming to Glasgow for holiday, which I find peculiar in itself, and Siobhan questioned but sounded more matter of fact that our town is still under a curse. It's nice they agreed to do the Winter Solstice ceremony with us, but I also got the feeling she has more to tell us." She looked at Judy. "Since that phone call, I have felt uneasy. Fearful to be exact and anxious of what Siobhan will have to say when she gets here two days from now," Latrice stated.

"So bottom line, we need to find this tome," Daniel stated.

"I feel bad that William isn't here," Judy said.

"I fear if we mention Anna's name again, he'll split into two," Daniel said. "However, maybe he'll help in other ways while we do the bigger stuff. I'll have him check Laurie's house again for the black book. It's gotta be somewhere."

Judy had another bright idea. "Well, at least invite him to go with us to Glasgow for Christmas shopping. We all need a break from this madness."

"What if one of us can't go?" Jeremy asked. Judy gave him a stern look to suggest that was not even an option.

"Sorry I asked. Stupid me," Jeremy retorted.

Chapter 6

THE BLACK BOOK

Glistening snowflakes slowly fell upon Glasgow's bustling walkways. Although it was cloudy, the sun peeked through to display its rays from time to time. While walking along the busy streets, bagpipes could be heard towards the town's centre. Business owners stood at their entrances, giving a warm greeting and announcing their store sales.

"This place is amazing!" Judy said. She couldn't get enough of the buildings, the shops, the noise. To Judy, it was beautiful, like a string orchestra playing Mozart's Concerto no. 6 in E-flat Major. She enjoyed breathing in the captivating atmosphere.

"We're acting like tourists, but I don't care. It feels good to go Christmas shopping without having to worry about time," Brandon said.

"Exactly! I think the last time we were here was two years ago. We never got the opportunity to relax and enjoy the scenery. We always had to rush home. I remember we got back to Beith too late, and we were in a line of cars just outside Beith. We couldn't afford a hotel, so we slept in the car until dawn," Judy said.

Normally there would be a moment of sadness remembering those days, but it was a past story. Something no one in Beith would hopefully ever have to experience again.

"I've heard people going through that. Crazy, I tell ye," Daniel said.

"OK. Enough of that! Let's focus on what you're getting me for Christmas," Latrice stated.

"I think William picked your name out of the drawing," Judy said.

"Crap. You allowed him to stay home, so now I cannae find out what he's getting me!" Latrice said to Judy.

"You're such a brat. Keep it up and I'll suggest to William to give you coal!" Judy laughed.

"Anyone else getting hungry?" Brandon asked. He rubbed his stomach while eyeing the café across the cobblestone road.

"Are you serious? We just had a huge, authentic Scottish breakfast at Jeremy's house. It's only been two hours!" Latrice exclaimed. She couldn't believe what she was hearing.

"Yeah, don't tell my mum that, or she'll think she will have to make more for next time," Jeremy said, panicked. He shook his head and looked at Daniel. Daniel quietly responded with a smirk. Latrice looked around and caught the eye of a spiritual shop, The Lion, Witch, and Wardrobe, and got Judy's attention.

"Let's go in there," Latrice said as she pointed at the store. Then she noticed the guys didn't want any part of it. "For goodness' sake, boys! Go eat!" The guys darted out to escape their grasp.

Judy and Latrice walked in and were immediately welcomed by a woman in a long, taupe wool sweater with a Celtic design, black leggings, and black wool boots.

"Welcome, lassies. Is there anything in particular yer lookin' for?" the owner asked.

"Actually, we are Druids, and we're looking for an ancient tome. A white book perhaps. Something to counter evil spells," Latrice mentioned.

"Interesting. Forgive me, but I took you as a witch," the owner said.

"Why would you assume that? I mean, I'm both, but what made you say that?" Latrice inquired.

"You have the tri-mark on your neck," the owner explained.

"I totally forgot about that, but good eye, ma'am," Latrice said. Both she and Judy were impressed by the owner's attention to detail. They looked at each other and silently agreed that they felt right at home.

"OK, back to your inquiry. One of the greatest tomes of white magic was stolen about a year ago. We looked diligently through our camera footage, but it didn't catch the thief. We put out reports, but we all know the police won't care about finding a book," the owner said.

Latrice asked, "Do you have maybe any books on protection, symbols, things like that?"

With a slight snide grin, the owner responded, "Hmm, to get spirits back to the dead perhaps?"

Latrice looked embarrassed, her face flushed. "Geez, does everyone know about Beith?"

"Well, the councillor did make an announcement about it," Judy stated.

While Judy and Latrice were looking around, a gentleman in a wheelchair came from the back room.

"Ahh, don't worry, lass. The missus here will do anything to help ye," the gentleman said. His enthusiastic demeanour brightened the room.

"This handsome gentleman is my partner, Phil, but friends call him Whippy," the owner said.

While pinching her butt and giving her a cheeky grin, he responded, "And this sexy woman is my wife, Crystal." Crystal bent down to kiss him, and he grabbed her butt. They were both slender and blue eyed. Whippy had short, blondish-brown hair, and she had long, wavy brown hair.

"Your diabetes actin' up, love?" Crystal asked.

"Yeah, I'll be OK as usual," Whippy said, smiling back to his wife.

"You two are so cute. I hope to have what you have someday," Judy said.

"Yer too kind, lass. Oh, trust me. We have had our ups and downs, but we get through it all right. Well, he doesn't have a choice." Crystal laughed.

Whippy swatted her butt, and said, "I'm goin' to head to the back." He looked at Judy and Latrice, and said, "I hope you find what yer lookin' for."

"Thanks, Whippy. Feel better," Judy said. Latrice smiled as she watched Whippy roll away in his wheelchair. Latrice looked at Crystal, and Crystal already knew what she was going to say.

"Oh, lass. No need for concern. He has a long road ahead of him, but he's going to be OK. I promise you. You must have had something similar happen in your life."

"You can say that," Latrice said. She stood in a daze for a moment, then shook it off. She snapped back to her normal demeanour.

"Ah, Ms. Crystal, what do you know about ritualists?" Latrice asked frankly.

"Oh child!" She gently directed the girls to the back room. "There are some things that shouldn't be mentioned in public, and that is one of them," Crystal whispered. Whippy overhead the conversation and had to put in his two pence about it.

"Listen to her. Those religious zealots think they know what is best for their religion and that any deviation from it is evil. You lot don't look evil to me. It's all about control, and when they don't have it, they'll do whatever it takes to get it. It's just not a topic for public discussion."

"That is so weird. I'm not going to be afraid of some religious zealot, as you called it, to getting in the way of doing what I need to do for Beith!" Latrice exclaimed.

"I understand you completely and couldn't agree more. However, don't put all the weight on your shoulders, lass. There are some people who are just too powerful for one to bear," Crystal said. Crystal looked at Latrice with affection as if she was her own child.

"I know. It's just we are exhausted." Latrice sighed. "I appreciate you talking with us and helping us, though."

"Of course, child. Now! As the sayin' goes, 'Whit's fur ye'll no go by ye.' Just know, things will fall into place when they need to. And feel free to continue to look about the store," Crystal said lovingly.

"I'll try not to worry as much. Thanks again, Ms. Crystal," Latrice replied.

"You're very welcome, lass," Crystal said. She smiled and went into the back room.

While Judy and Latrice were looking around, Judy suddenly stopped and shouted.

"Do you hear that?!"

"More bagpipes!" Latrice exclaimed. They rushed to the window next to the front door and watched the Royal Regiment in their green tartans and red jackets, tall black feather bonnet, their plaids draped over their shoulders, and the sporran in the front just below the waistline. And of course, the most important part, the bagpipes. They were playing "Scotland the Brave." It was as though Judy and Latrice were hearing it for the first time as tears filled their eyes. They realised they had missed out on so much in their lives saving Beith. When the drums started playing, their hearts blossomed to not just being Druids, but remembering the most important part of them. Being Scottish. It was something to be very proud of and to never be forgotten.

While still looking out the window, hearing the bagpipes dissipating into the distance, Latrice calmly said,

"Promise me from time to time you'll tell me, Judy, that I'm more than just a high priestess."

Judy knew it had nothing to do with narcissism but about their heritage and not losing part of who they were in the midst of the evils in Beith. Judy turned to Latrice, and said quietly, "You are a warrior, Latrice. You are rigid at times, but that's only because you care so much for so many. You seek truth at every turn, and you are a natural-born leader. You try at nothing because you just do. You are my friend, and I'm proud to be your ovate, your friend, the cheerleader." They both chuckled. "But I can be that way because of the confidence you bring to the grove and the community. That, Latrice, makes you wholeheartedly Scottish."

They embraced in a hug.

"Thank you. I needed that," Latrice said calmly.

"Good. Now snap out of it, will ye?! I need the abrasive Latrice back!" Judy exclaimed.

"Oh! You think yer funny, do ye?" Latrice laughed. Just then, Crystal came out to check on them.

"Is everything all right?"

"Yes. We were just admiring the Royal Regiment and the bagpipes," Latrice replied.

"Ah yes. The joy to my ears," Crystal responded happily.

"We would like to get these," Judy said. Judy and Latrice placed their items on the counter.

"Lovely choices. It's always good to stay on top of proper spells and the like. I hope it helps in your time of need," Crystal said. Judy and Latrice paid, and they made their exchanges and said their goodbyes.

"I wonder what the guys are up to?" Judy asked.

"Eating and scheming. What else?" Latrice replied. She and Judy laughed and headed to another store.

While Brandon, Jeremy, and Daniel ate their pastries and drank their coffees, Daniel got a text from William.

I'm having a Christmas party on Sunday. Don't bring anything but empty bellies!

"Hey, I just got a text from William. He's having a party at his house on Sunday and says not to bring anything," Daniel said.

"Sounds like my kind of party!" Brandon said. Both Jeremy and Daniel looked at him appalled.

"Anyway, I say we go. He probably has a new shield or collector item thing to show us," Daniel said.

"I think he's feeling guilty for not helping us," Jeremy retorted.

"Cut him some slack. He's still our mate and has every right to feel like he does," Daniel replied.

"True. Maybe he can help us in other ways, like research or something," Brandon suggested.

Daniel pondered for a moment.

"Oh hell. He's got that contemplating look. I see the cogwheels turning. Wait for it. Wait for it," Jeremy taunted.

"Wheesht! Ye jobbie!" They all laughed. "Yes, as a matter of fact, there is a piece of information we are still missing." Daniel whispered, "I think it's time for William to help search the black book."

"Where do you think it is?" Jeremy asked.

"Not sure but I don't think we searched Laurie's room thoroughly enough," Daniel replied.

Daniel picked up his mobile and called William.

"William. Hey, bud. We will all be there Sunday." Jeremy rolled his eyes, hearing Daniel. "I do have a favour, though. Would you be willing to go to Laurie's house and get all her books? Yes? Awesome. Thanks, mate!" Daniel ended the call and went back to drinking his coffee as if nothing happened.

"Oh, you're slick. Well played, my friend," Jeremy said.

As William made his way to Laurie's house, all he could think about was Anna. With one hand on the steering wheel and the other balled in a fist, propping his head from the side of the window, he wondered if it was time to face his fears. He wasn't some demon slayer, but the very least he could do was help his friends. Maybe Daniel was right. It wasn't about the group really but all of Beith and everyone's safety.

William wasn't ready to pledge himself to the group just yet, but he had convinced himself to at least help when the time presented itself.

He arrived at Ms. Turner's house. William noticed that she had boxes on the porch and the boot of her car opened. He pulled over to the side of the road and went to see what was going on.

"Hello, Ms. Turner. Not sure if you remember me but—" William started to say before being interrupted.

"Yes. Hello, William. How are you holdin' up, dear laddie?" Ms. Turner said with a smile.

"I'm fine, ma'am." He looked around, and then asked, "Are ye movin' somewhere?"

"I'm still debating. This house is too big for me now. A small flat would do me just fine really. Honestly, I have been havin' terrible night terrors about Laurie. I know she's dead, but part of me felt like something malevolent was lingering here. I figured if I removed everythin' but pictures, maybe the bad dreams would fade," Ms. Turner said. Her facial expression showed signs of exasperation and desperation for answers, and she felt as though she was out of options.

"Do you mind if I look through the boxes? Daniel asked me to look for a particular book," William said.

"I think I know which one you are looking for. Be leery, William. It seems like that book is not for the faint of heart," Ms. Turner stated. She gave him a fervid look, which made him want to recant his earlier thoughts of helping his mates. "It's in the boot, love," she said.

"I promise I will be ever so careful," William stated. He walked to the boot of her car and looked at the one box shoved into the back corner. He pulled the box towards him and opened it. There it was. The black book. The book of evil filled with enchantments, rituals, and the like that had caused Beith's mayhem. Just looking at the book made him have goosebumps. He took a deep breath, closed the box, and called Daniel.

"Mate, I have it," William said.

Judy and Latrice came in with shopping bags and sat on the side of Daniel. Daniel whispered, "William has it."

"Has what, and why are we whispering?" Latrice asked.

"William found the black book apparently," Jeremy said.

"Oh, OK. Tell him to take it to the warehouse," Latrice responded.

"You sound scared. What happened?" Daniel asked.

"Mate. This book is truly of demon origin, and just looking at it is scary. I can't explain it," William stated. His breathing was becoming erratic.

"Latrice said you can't bring it into anyone's house. She said take it to the old Willow Warehouse in South Beith," Daniel stated.

"OK," William said.

"Latrice will know what to do. We should be back from Glasgow in about an hour," Daniel said.

Latrice smiled at Daniel's response.

"Good! Because this thing is creepin' me out!" William exclaimed. They hung up. William was hoping they would get to the warehouse sooner than later.

He grabbed the box and put it in the boot of his car. The images of a raised cover that resembled the dead in hell, along with serpents on each of the corners and a reversed pentagram at the centre, made his heart pound in fear. It was becoming very clear what Anna and the rest of the dead had gone went through. What they were going through. He looked back at Ms. Turner.

"Thank you," William said.

"That thing and along with whatever else is what killed Laurie. Don't let it devour you and your mates, William," Ms. Turner said.

"Trust me. It won't!" William exclaimed.

Ms. Turner went back inside to gather more boxes. The house seemed brighter as if a huge and pungent heavy mass had left her house. She thought that tonight she would finally get some much-needed sleep. However, as soon as she had her blissful thoughts, they were instantaneously clouded by fear for William. For his mates. It was then she realised that whatever evil was part of that book, wanted something or someone in particular. She packed up the rest of boxes and dropped them off at the local thrift store.

Meanwhile, William reached the southern end of Beith. The old Willow Warehouse, a one-time armament depot that was abandoned after the walkout of 2045. Over three hundred workers were forgotten about and weren't paid for over three months. The Salic Company, who produced the majority of the ammunitions for the United Kingdom's military, was bought out Lindose. Lindose went to inspect all warehouses and found a functional warehouse with no one in it but one person. Daniel Willow. When asked where everyone was, Daniel explained what happened. Daniel had every worker's file, and Lindose contacted every single worker and compensated them with six months' wages. Although many were pleased, the workers had already found new jobs or were reluctant to work for them in fear of being forgotten about again.

There were twenty warehouses in total. Currently there were three abandoned warehouses; the rest had been removed due to new property owners using the area for cultivation.

William noticed that there wasn't a lock on the side door. It was likely that Latrice or someone had been there before, hence why she suggested this place. The two large sliding doors were locked by an old, rusted chain with a lock. He walked in and saw a few stainless-steel tables that looked like they had been pushed around at one time. The floors and walls on the inside were made of concrete, but the outside was a corrugated metal. There were two offices to the left. William put the box down and went to investigate the old offices. One had an old metal desk and leather chair, the other had the same and a black filing cabinet. He was disappointed to find nothing inside any of the drawers. Above the large sliding doors was a partially broken vent, and towards the opposite side of the building was one window. William walked over to the window to just get a glimpse of the view.

Squeak went one of the tables.

William quickly turned about but didn't see anything. He slowly walked over to the table where he placed the box. When he got to the table, a raven cawed from the ground. William jumped, his heart racing. The raven jumped onto the table, looked at William, and then flew out of the broken vent.

William wasn't having any more of this. He called Daniel, but there was no reception. He then went outside to try his mobile again, and when he went outside, a large magnitude of ravens was on the ground. Some hopping, some squawking, some on top of the bushes. He called Daniel. No answer. He called again and again. No answer. After a few moments, Daniel called back.

"We are almost there. You OK, mate?" Daniel asked.

"NO! I'm not OK in the slightest! This black book is no joke! You won't believe this!" William yelled. He took a picture of all the ravens and sent it to Daniel. William's caption for the pictures was *They arrived with the book*.

Daniel looked at the picture and knew something was about to happen again. It seemed wherever that book was, evil followed. As if the book were the new altar the group would have to destroy. "What did Ms. Turner say? Anything?" Daniel asked.

"She told me that whatever evil is with this book is what killed Laurie and for us to be cautious basically. She seemed scared by it and might move if she doesn't get any sleep," William said. He tried to remember all that Ms. Turner said, but by the time he got to the warehouse, he couldn't recollect much.

The group finally arrived, and they could see William in complete distress. They ran over to him, and then Latrice asked him to show her the book. Everyone became a little apprehensive being at the warehouse when they saw all the ravens. William wasn't kidding. The scene was out of a horror movie. They walked inside, and Latrice saw the box on the table. She slowly walked towards it. "Caw!" a raven sounded while sitting on the broken vent above them. It made them leap out of their skin. William expressed to them, "See why I don't want to be here?"

Latrice opened the box and looked inside to verify that it was actually the black book. When she did, she was immediately pushed back. A glowing, shifting eye locked onto Latrice. She immediately closed the lid.

"Well, well. Someone is looking for you." She turned to Judy. "We need to put this somewhere, and I need to put a protection spell on it. Seems like a demon is trying to take hold of the book. If it falls within the realm of the netherworld, we won't be able to free the dead. Especially if we also can't find the ancient tome needed to free them." She looked to William. "Is there something in these other rooms where we can place this?"

William pointed to one of the offices.

"There's an old cabinet in there."

"Perfect!" she exclaimed.

She placed the box inside one of the cabinet drawers. Since she was the only witch present, she was the only one who could conduct the spell. Latrice had fire appear in the palm of her hands. She whispered her chant; the group could hear something like *Only those of the light may approach*. Certain words together meant certain things. Latrice shielded the book so that only she, a higher Druid, or God himself would be the one that could touch it. Judy knew the book had to be protected, but why this particular spell?

"What did you do?"

Latrice didn't hesitate to answer.

"Keeping all of you safe! I don't want the demons using anyone to attempt to get that book!"

As they headed towards their cars, William noticed that the ravens were gone.

"Look! Her spell must be working because the ravens are gone!"

Latrice looked and noticed one was sitting on top of a shrub. She stared at it from a distance, and said, "Shoo!" The raven gawked and flew away. Brandon was quite impressed.

"Her witchy abilities are awesome!"

Judy gave him a wee smack to imply that now was not the time.

"We are exhausted, but we have a few matters to talk about before tomorrow," Latrice stated.

Jeremy immediately texted his mum forewarning her he'd be home soon and comin' with a crowd. Of course, Margorie was pleased and started cooking.

"Looks like we're going to my house. My mum knows we're comin'."

"Thanks, Jeremy!" everyone said. Going to Jeremy's house now and staying up a little longer for one of Latrice's meetings made it that much more tolerable.

It wasn't long before Nixia located the black book. Soon it would be in her hands, and she would have perfect favour with her father again. Nixia was instantly transported to her father's throne room. With a gleam in his eyes, the dark king walked up to Nixia.

"I feel that you have something I want. Where is it?"

Nixia proudly gleamed back, and stated, "It's in a warehouse on the south side of Beith, Father."

He paced intently back and forth, thinking how to add to his plan. He tapped his fingers together, scheming. Then an idea came to mind.

"Keep the black book where it is for now. It seems like those Druid brats aren't going to do anything with it until they find an ancient tome. We have to beat them to it! Because if, I mean, when we have both, we get to torture their spirits while the dead remain as they are."

Nixia was happy to get to earth again. Feasting on living flesh and tormenting those that got in her way made her feel exuberant.

"Oh, it would be my absolute pleasure, Father!"

The dark king was very pleased and trusted her with the second mission.

"Excellent! Make your preparations and search assiduously before heading up there but do make haste. We don't want to risk both books falling in their dirty little Druid hands!"

Nixia bowed and vanished.

The group arrived at Jeremy's house, and it wasn't long before fun meals appeared on the countertops.

The guys wasted zero time digging into the greasy deliciousness of pizza, cheesy bread, and chicken wings.

Latrice looked at Jeremy's mum with admiration. She took care of all of them at any given time, and all she wanted was to be helpful to their mission. Latrice walked up beside her, and whispered, "Ms. Margorie. Can I talk to you for a moment, please?"

She finished placing sodas in the refrigerator and walked with Latrice to the back room.

"I never want you to think that we take advantage of you. We appreciate you so much. When we are here, we know we will be cared for, listened to, and given advice when needed. Honestly, I'm not sure what we would do without you. So I saw this and thought of you. This is how I see you. Well, we see you."

Latrice handed her a little red box. Margorie's hands were shaking from Latrice's words. She opened the box, and there was a 24k gold necklace and a golden angel holding a child. Margorie was at a loss for words and gestured to have Latrice put the necklace on her.

"It's beautiful! So lovely of you to think of me!"

Latrice then pulled her wallet from her purse and proceeded to take out a substantial amount of cash. Margorie placed her hand over Latrice's and refused to accept.

"No, love. I do what I can because you and your friends, including my own son, does more to save Beith than any adult. How did saving Beith become your responsibility over being a teenager? All of you have sacrificed so much and allowed Beith to be your priority. It is the very least I can do."

Latrice smiled and hugged her. Margorie couldn't help but look at the angel. Latrice then said, "Don't be surprised if you just happen to see a few hundred pounds in a kitchen drawer as a token of our appreciation. I mean, I do have my witchy ways of making things appear."

"Oh dear. I guess I cannae stop ye now, can I?" Margorie said. She shook her head and accepted all of Latrice's acts of kindness.

They walked back towards the kitchen, and Jeremy gave his mum a strange look.

"What was that about?"

Margorie smiled and showed everyone her necklace.

"Latrice said this is how you all see me."

Everyone stopped eating and approached the counter to look at the golden trinket. Judy was awed, while the guys thought it was cool. Their reactions were different, but they all agreed that it fit, especially in the current situation.

Latrice decided to start the informal meeting to address who was going to find Julia and when.

"Continue to eat. I'm hoping this will be quick actually. First of all, when would be a good time to go to Dunino Den? We also need to know who, besides myself, is available to go?"

Judy took a sip of her Fanta, and replied, "You know I'll go."

Brandon perked up.

"I'll go if she goes. Plus, you two shouldn't go alone. The spirits only know who this woman is or what she's capable of doing once she sees us!"

Latrice agreed, and asked, "So when is a good time? I figure we gather as much information we can in the meantime, take a break, and go a day before Winter Solstice."

Judy and Brandon looked at the other and nodded to suggest no issues.

"What are you going to ask Julia if you find her?" Daniel asked.

Latrice didn't really know herself.

"Honestly, not quite sure. That's why I think we need a day to prepare. We definitely need to know about Anna's rune and find out about the tome. I'm sure from there we'll acquire more information."

Latrice watched as everyone was eating, laughing, and carrying on. She realised this was her life, and she had great friends to help her. To help Beith. She didn't need to experience what teenagers did. Looking at her friends, she knew she just needed them.

Chapter 7

JULIA

Judy, Latrice, and Brandon made it to the car park and were on edge to seek out Julia. Nighttime in Scotland, especially this night, was exceptionally colder. Dunino Den was illuminated by the full moon, and the fog hovered and spread across the den's landscape, adding to the mystery of their adventure.

"Why haven't we ever come here during the day?" Judy inquired.

Latrice agreed it was an excellent question, but she didn't have an answer. Dunino Den was home to ancient Druids. Many face carvings were etched in or protruded from many stones. Moon and sun signs could be found throughout, and visitors had placed small gifts, messages, and coins to loved ones that had passed on.

They started at the long, narrow walkway that suddenly merged to a steep, twenty-five-stone staircase. When they reached the bottom, they noticed many of the offerings, and a man's face with long hair and a long beard shown on the stone above them.

"What do you think that is?" Judy asked.

To everyone's surprise, Brandon had mentioned Dunino Den was home to ancient Druid and pagan worshippers. So back 4000 BC or earlier, depending on who was predominant, Druids or pagans, the face could be either the Dagda or Zeus.

"Wow! I'm impressed!" Latrice said.

"If we are Druids, then we should know something about our history," Brandon stated.

"Very true," Judy agreed. She looked at him with admiration. However, now was not the time to be giddy over Brandon's moment of scholarly intuition. They needed to find Julia.

They took a sharp right and continued on the narrow walkway. An owl hooted, alerting other animals that they were nearby. Judy nearly leapt out of her skin, not expecting it to be so loud. She caught her breath, and soon after the walkway became a little wider.

"Kind of odd that we are seeing mist when we have a full moon. I think we might have found our witch," Latrice stated.

"I didn't realise you were studying to be a meteorologist," Brandon said.

"Ha ha. Very funny. I think we all have been down this road before when trying to look for the altar," Latrice retorted.

"Yeah, don't remind me," Judy added.

"Oddly, at this time of night, it doesn't feel eerie," Latrice noted.

"Maybe your witchy ways make this feel like home, but I'm creeped out!" Brandon said.

"Oh, someone has all the jokes tonight. Watch it, Brandon, before I turn you into a frog!" Latrice said. She looked him dead in the eyes to express she was serious but then tricked him and started laughing. Brandon took a deep breath and chuckled.

"Too funny. Both of you. But I'm cold so let's find her already!" Judy exclaimed.

Just then Brandon tucked his torch into his back pocket and rubbed Judy's arms. She closed her eyes, took in a deep breath, and smiled. Brandon was always attentive when it came to Judy. Before the jubilee, Brandon had been very awkward around girls and didn't know how to approach them. However, with Judy it was just natural and felt right. Judy turned around and hugged him. They held each other for a few moments until Latrice interrupted.

"Oh my gosh you two! Quit yer snoggin'! We have a witch to find!"

"Right," Brandon replied. He gave a quick intimidated look, feeling like his mum had just scolded him.

"Look! There!" Latrice announced.

As they got closer, the mist was closer to the ground, and it was centre within the circle of stones. The stones were tall and hollow. Some had been torn down due to age, but out of the ten that were standing, seven were in relatively decent shape. Within the circle's centre were seven square stones, in a circle, resembling a firepit. On each stone, there was a mark. Judy and Brandon watched Latrice as she inspected the stones.

"Judy. Look. Tell me what you see," Latrice said.

"I see symbols but not sure what they mean," Judy replied.

"These symbols are separated. The symbol we have seen where all of these are one," Latrice stated.

"Yes! Anna's protection rune!" Judy exclaimed.

"We hit the jackpot!" Brandon said excitedly.

"Let's not jump the gun. We still need to find Julia," Latrice said.

Adjacent to where they were standing, a shadowy figure appeared.

"Oh, hell no! Not this shadow business again!" Brandon declared. He moved back, placing his hands out to protect both Judy and Latrice. The shadow figure took a step closer. This time, the shadow was more defined, having long hair and wearing pants, wellies, and a coat.

"Julia?" Judy questioned. Her voice was not boisterous but more like a desperate cry. She hoped that they had finally found her.

The shadowy figure turned around and disappeared. Brandon turned around to face Judy and yelled. Judy and Latrice turned around to see what he was goin' on about and saw the shadowy figure.

"Who wants to know?" Julia asked, staring at them.

"Is that your thing? Scaring people?" Latrice snarled.

"It keeps the drifters away. And yes, lass, I am Julia," she said.

All of them stared at her, and Julia looked confused.

"It's a good thing Daniel isn't here. Ms. Julia is a mirror image of Anna," Brandon said.

"Well, I'm Latrice. These are my friends, Judy and Brandon, and we are Druids from Beith. We really need to talk to you about Anna. Your daughter," Latrice stated.

Without hesitation, Julia said, "This way."

She turned, and everyone followed her to another stone structure not too far away. When she pushed two stones simultaneously, a large stone moved, and it led downward into her lair. Brandon saw this, and whispered to Judy, "Is it wise to go into a witch's lair?"

Judy elbowed him gently in the gut, turned to him wide-eyed, and whispered back, "Shut up!"

All of them reached the bottom of the structure. Latrice, Judy, and Brandon looked around with amazement. The walls and floor were all stone; it was one-story tall and the size of two studio flats shaped close to an *E*.

The first indent immediately to the right was a small sitting area with a small round table and captain-style camping chairs. Along the wall were pictures of various stone ruins, forest pictures during the summer and autumn, and one of an infant child. In between the pictures were candlestick holders that could hold pillar candles that were five centimetres in diameter.

"Ms. Julia. Who is this?" Brandon asked while pointing at the infant in the picture. Julia turned around and looked, tilting her head slightly, and smiled.

"My sweet Anna," she replied.

The second indent was wider and fit two twin-sized beds, and behind them stood some shelving. Looking towards the back and right, you could see a makeshift shower and toilet. There was also a small area with a hand pump for water and a bucket underneath it. The third indent was the kitchen area. Dry herbs were hanging along the wall, vegetables were in a wrought-iron rack below them, and on the adjacent wall on another iron rack were plants and other rare items in jars. They were likely used for spells. Below the rack of vegetables was a long wooden table. Farthest back was a stone oven, and the smoke was redirected through a vent that led to a manhole at a nearby road. Opposite the kitchen was a washing area with a hanging rack.

"I have so many questions!" Latrice stated. Looking around the place, she was amazed by how Julia had made this hidden gem her home.

"Please, let's get acquainted," Julia said. They sat in the sitting area while Julia handed them each some hot chocolate.

"How long have you been here, and why this place?" Judy asked. She sat in the chair, sipping her hot chocolate like a child waiting for a bedtime story.

Julia was a very slender woman with long brown, scraggily locks, sea-blue eyes, and oddly long lashes. Her demeanour was mysterious yet relaxed.

"I'll start with the second part of your question. This place was one of many transient Druid homes throughout Scotland. Christians, specifically Catholics, rebuked the Druid way of life, pushing Druids out of their forest homes, especially County Skye. Catholics were the majority in Scotland for centuries, so it was common to have a major influence with the government. Thankfully, the government got tired of the Catholics' antics and believed it was time to just coexist. It was very popular for Druids to live upon the earth, and the same was true for witches. Yet the Druids were the ones targeted, for a lack of a better term anyway. After the government stopped listening to the religious 'Karens,' the Catholics implemented the ritualists," Julia explained.

"Father Mac told us about them. They basically study other practices to ensure they won't harm the Catholic Church," Brandon stated.

"More like infect. The Catholic sect that developed the ritualist, from what I've come to understand, is looking to eliminate other religious cultures and have the church be the only religion," Julia stated.

"That's absurd!" Judy yelled. "Druids are friendly, kind, and welcoming! I mean, look at us!"

"You're really sounding like that now, aren't ye?" Brandon laughed.

"Sorry, just sounds so daft to me," Judy said, trying to calm down.

Julia continued. "Although the ritualists really haven't intruded on my life, I still lack trust in many areas. Which brings me to the first part of your question. I have been down here for sixteen years. But before I begin, would you like more hot chocolate? Or perhaps some tea?" she asked. It was very unlikely she had many guests in her dwelling, and she wasn't sure how to interact like a hostess should. Although she was polite, hospitality wasn't her strong suit, since it wasn't practiced often. Latrice, Judy, and Brandon nodded and appreciated Julia's kindness.

"Right, so, sixteen years I have lived as a witch rather than a Druid. I wanted to help people through my magic rather than from the spirits. I'm not saying that in a negative light, it's just a preference," Julia said. Both Latrice and Judy looked at each other when Julia said "help people through magic." Their thoughts were in sync, and they felt that Julia was the one who had put the rune on Anna.

"I understand," Latrice noted.

"My understanding is that many of my ancestors were Druids," Julia started, but then she paused. She looked as if she were about to have an anxiety attack.

"Ms. Julia! Are you all right?" Judy asked.

"Forgive me. I know you are here about Anna, but I must tell you this in hopes things will make sense. I became a witch sixteen years ago because I wanted revenge on the man who raped me. No religion, deity, spirit, or otherwise was going to get in the way of that. I cursed him and cast a spell that would lead to his tragic end. After I did the spell, two days later, he was in a fatal accident," Julia explained.

Brandon tapped Judy on the arm.

"Yeah. I think Scotland Yard is still trying to understand that case. It happened out on A68. The cars simultaneously just crashed into each other as though everyone blanked out at the same time," he said.

"True. Realising that my curse caused other people to die, I have never done a curse since. My spells, like I mentioned earlier, are for helping others. Healing wounds, things like that," Julia finished. Latrice didn't waste time bringing up the rune.

"So good spells like putting protection runes on people, right?"

"No. That dabbles a little bit into necromancy. And that, young lass, is something no one should mess with!" Julia exclaimed.

"So you didn't use any magic to have a protection rune branded into Anna's arm?" Latrice asked.

"No, I know how it's done, but a witch can't do it alone," Julia stated.

Latrice looked at Julia shocked.

"OK. We are definitely coming back to that but let me ask this. Do you have any idea what has been goin' on in Beith? The curse and how Agnes allowed the shadow from the netherworld to kill over seventy people in a span of fifty years as a sacrifice so she could have high priestess powers?" Latrice asked. She was very direct and was getting impatient. Something wasn't adding up. Julia's eyes glazed over, and she was in shock. Brandon sat up in his chair and became enraged.

"Ms. Julia! Everyone knows about Beith! I know you haven't lived in here for so long that you don't know what's goin' on in the world! Don't lie!"

"Stop, Brandon! Latrice! We are in her home. Remember, she is Anna's mother. We haven't told her what happened to Anna," Judy exclaimed.

Weeping, Julia could hardly get the words out.

"I know what she did to my Anna. I read the papers when Agnes was sentenced."

Brandon slowly relaxed in his chair, and they all waited to see what Julia was going to say next.

"Yes. I have very much been in denial. I trusted Agnes to watch over my baby girl because I still couldn't handle the fact that I was raped and left alone. Agnes was the only family I knew of, and she promised she would protect her. Please tell me what happened," Julia begged. She didn't plead in a dramatic way, but she needed to hear the story so she could have closure.

"Are you sure?" Judy asked.

"I'm sure," Julia said. Now she was waiting for the story, nestled in her chair. Judy explained how Anna had found love with William, and when they were at the jubilee, the shadow came and took Anna and their teacher. Latrice and Brandon dolefully sat listening as Judy reiterated the events from that tragic day.

"What did Agnes do when the shadow took Anna?" Julia asked. Julia seemed full of hate for Agnes. The same hate that many of Beith felt for her.

"Ah, she really didn't do anything other than just stand in shock. It was then we knew Agnes did something to cause the shadow to take Anna. And many others," Judy said.

Julia sat in silence. Latrice, Judy, and Brandon shifted their eyes, looking at each other, then back at Julia. An awkward silence hovered over them, and Judy still wasn't finished because she needed to tell Julia about the current events. Judy looked at Julia and noticed her eyes were now sharp and not bright like before.

"Ah, Latrice!" Judy exclaimed, pointing at Julia.

"A shok um ay day!" Latrice yelled as she thrusted her hands forward, casting a rebuking spell. Julia flipped back from her chair, and whatever spirit was present faded away above them. Brandon ran over to help Julia off the ground.

"You are a very powerful witch!" Julia stated. She rubbed her neck and back a little bit but indicated she was OK.

With jubilant pride, Judy added, "She's also our high priestess!"

"What just happened?" Brandon asked. He looked at everyone like someone had better give him an answer right then.

"I think it was the spirit of anger. You, too, are a powerful witch," Latrice said. She paused for a moment, then said, "That's why you have been keeping yourself secluded from society, isn't it?" Latrice was fixated on Julia, and Julia wasn't about to entertain any battles to determine who was the dominant witch. That had already been made quite clear.

"Correct. I can't risk it as you clearly saw," Julia replied.

"Let's talk about how a witch cannot cast a protection rune by themselves. The rocks outside had symbols on them that match the ones on Anna's arm. Only not separate but all inclusive," Latrice stated. Judy pulled out her phone and showed Julia the picture.

"That is an interesting grouping of the runes. The lotus represents December thirteenth through the twenty-ninth in the Druid calendar. The triangles that are embedded in the stones out at the altar crag represent direction. North, south, east, and west. However, in this picture, the triangles here are more like valknuts, which symbolize the transition of life through death. Some believe that it's birth, to death, and back to life again. The arrows represent bravery and point outward meaning away from the main symbol. Oddly, the diamond with no knots is strange, but out of this whole tattoo, this is the only part that represents protection. So in actuality, the tattoo is not a protection rune. It was a warning. Had she only represented the diamond symbol on her arm, it would presumably be a protection rune. In this case, it was meant to warn the barer about what is to come," Julia explained.

"All this time, we thought it was for protection but was something totally different," Latrice exclaimed. She felt angry at herself for not knowing this earlier. Everyone saw that message loud and clear on Latrice's face.

"We should have researched better! Maybe we could have done something, and when I say we, I really mean me. I could have done something to stop the shadow from getting Anna!"

Julia got up and hugged Latrice. Then she stood back, still holding on to Latrice's arms and gently told her, "It is no one's fault but Agnes's. There is no way anyone would have known what to do. You, all of you, did what you could for Anna, and for that I am grateful," Julia said.

They sat quietly for a few moments, shocked at what the rune meant. Julia then went into explaining about the spell.

"The reason why a witch needs to also participate is to solidify the protection runes. It would look like handwritten words surrounding the runes. It sounds easy enough, but in actuality if the ritual is not performed correctly, it can bring in evil rather than repel it. Think of it like a beacon that alerts the evil spirit that the person having the rune is of interest to them. The spirits in turn will believe that the rune, incorrectly placed in this case, was meant for them to find. Bottom line, whoever read the incantation for this rune, one, did not have a witch present and, two, had no clue what they were doing," she firmly stated.

"I wonder if this person was reading from an ancient tome?" Latrice asked.

"Do you know how long Anna had that rune?" Julia asked.

"Not sure really because we really started talking to her only after she came back to school. She was homeschooled before coming back due to being in shock after losing her dad to the shadow. So maybe about six months or more, why?" Judy inquired.

"I'm not too familiar with the Druid ways, but I can say that it was a Druid that did this spell. I think they thought they could do both parts. Oh, there are actually three tomes, and where they are exactly is a mystery. One of them I found at a bookstore, but it was later stolen from me," Julia stated.

Latrice and Judy looked at each other, remembering what Crystal had told them about their stolen tome.

"Another would possibly be in a sacred place, like the Vatican or hidden archives, and the third is likely with the person who put this rune on Anna," Julia said.

"I have another question, if that is OK?" Latrice asked.

"Absolutely!" Julia replied.

"We have the black book. How do we destroy it?" Latrice asked.

"Ah, more importantly, how did you come upon having it?" Julia inquired. She became very concerned for them.

"Laurie, Daniel's girlfriend, who also succumbed to the shadow, had it in her possession. She was a Druid," Latrice said.

"The black book should not be used by Druids, as that is for dark magic, which I'm sure you have seen. Druids rely on spirits of the earth, sea, and sky; whereas witches rely on dominion spirits. Good or bad. I'm sure you have all heard of the power of three. There is some truth to that as you would need three witches to disenchant the black book. Another way is to simply burn it. However, it would be best to disenchant and then burn it to ensure no remnants are left behind. Lastly, would be divine intervention," Julia suggested.

"Divine intervention? You mean God or one of his angels?" Brandon asked.

"Precisely," Julia confirmed.

"Well, before we destroy it, we do have to tell you what's been goin' on in Beith. We may have to use it in order to assist with our current dilemma," Latrice said.

"It would be best to find the tome, but what is going on?" Julia asked. From all three, there were deep sighs and some hesitation before giving Julia the agonizing news.

"Ms. Julia. Please brace yourself for this. Before Agnes was taken to Glasgow, those killed, technically, showed up at her house. In other words, the dead have returned from the netherworld, and one of them was Anna," Judy said.

There was a long pause. Julia stared at the floor a moment and then back at Judy and Latrice.

"I appreciate you all coming here and telling me all this. I cannae tell ye how wonderful it was to meet you, but something tells me it's not safe for you here. Remember, find the tome and you will allow the spirits to find peace."

Judy embraced Julia, and said, "Thank you, Julia. Anna would have been proud to have you as a mother had she known you."

Julia touched her heart and returned an appreciative smile. She then turned to the wall and pressed her hand three times upon a stone, and the top of her abode slid open. They walked up the stairs.

"If you take this path instead of the way you came, you will get to your vehicle quicker," Julia said.

They were grateful for the advice and said their last goodbyes. Little did Latrice, Judy, and Brandon know, it would be their very last goodbye.

Julia carefully returned to her dwelling, and with a wave of her hand, everything disappeared. She felt the darkness creeping back in and knew the last of her powers would be better used elsewhere.

A slender woman, wearing a black trench coat and blue heels with her hair in a bun and wearing librarian-style black-rimmed glasses asked the guard at the front desk to see Agnes Aird. There was no hesitation from the guard as she immediately called for an escort for the mysterious woman. They walked back, gates slamming closed as they reached each corridor. With her hands in her pockets, she walked steadily towards Agnes's pod, displaying a slight, cheeky grin. Agnes saw the woman coming.

She was confused, yet she managed to smile at the unknown visitor. The woman sat down and kept her poise and demeanour. She looked at Agnes and then looked at the guard, and asked, "I have an odd request, but may I please have her hairbrush or something of hers? I mean, let's face it. She may not be here much longer anyway."

The guard, as though in a trance, opened the pod and grabbed the brush from the small table and handed it to the woman.

"How dare you? Who are you, and why do you need anything of mine?" Agnes demanded.

The woman looked at the guard, and said, "Thank you." She rendered a smile, and then her facial expression turned cunning and devious when she looked at Agnes.

"You're not the only one that can invoke curses!"

Agnes looked at the woman with disgust. Paused. Her eyebrows rose, her mouth opened in shock, and her eyes widened.

"It can't be!"

"Oh, it is," the woman said sarcastically.

The woman smiled and told the guard she was ready to leave.

As she walked out of the building, she shape-shifted into her original self and disappeared as she walked down the sidewalk. The guard shook off whatever spell seemed to have consumed him and ran out the door after the woman.

He stopped halfway towards the street, constantly looking back and forth around the building, but he didn't see her. As the woman returned to her humble abode, her cauldron was already filled and bubbling with some eye of newt, a couple of bat wings, and a spider's venom sac. She then took the blade onto herself and drew blood from her hand and allowed each drop to splash into the cauldron. Last but not least, she added a few strands of Agnes's hair to the potent mixture. As the hair fell slowly upon the mixture, the water instantly turned into bluish liquid while the steam turned into white smoke. She took her blade and carved *AGNES* into the black candle. As she carved Agnes's name, she never thought this day would come. The promise she'd made to herself long ago would be broken. Of course, she was the only one that could break her own promise. She didn't owe an explanation to anyone.

After the woman prepared some last-minute spells, she began her incantations. She knew once she started, it would come back to her times three. She made it that way, making the evil brew. Soon she embraced the shroud of darkness and acceded to the curse.

The telephone rang at 3:04 a.m. Irene groggily answered. She was not expecting what she heard next. Her sister had died of a heart attack. Irene rose in her bed and began to cry. "Thank you. I'll contact you later about arrangements," Irene told the warden.

She slowly swung her legs over the side of the mattress and continued to cry. The tears were falling, but she was numb at the same time. All these years, Irene knew that Agnes kept so many secrets and hurt so many people. She thought finally, *It was well deserved.* Yet at the same time, it was her sister. They would chase each other around the house, be mischievous during Sunday school, pretend to be princesses waiting for their prince to rescue them. Irene wiped her tears away and was able to calm her thoughts. She looked at the clock, and the digital blue number brightly shone 3:48 a.m. She got up to check on Sabrina and was relieved to find Sabrina was in a deep sleep. Irene went downstairs and rang Daniel.

"Is everything OK, Auntie?" Daniel asked. He was on pins and needles thinking, something happened to her or Sabrina.

"Yes. However, I wanted to talk to you first before you heard it on the news. I just received a call from the warden at the police station. Your mother died of a heart attack earlier this morning," Irene said. Daniel didn't say anything. She only imagined he was in just as much shock as she was.

"Does Sabrina know?" Daniel asked.

"Not yet. I'll tell her when she wakes up," Irene said.

"I'm not sure how to feel right now," Daniel said.

"I understand. I think you are feeling anger, and plus you have stuff going on there that you're figuring out," Irene stated.

"Thanks for your understanding. I love you. Now I'm going back to bed." Daniel chuckled.

"OK, you." Irene laughed. "I'll talk to ye soon."

Daniel was in the guest room at Jeremy's house. He was thankful that Jeremy didn't start knocking on the door asking axiomatic questions. However, in a few hours, the whole gang was going to know. He had to mentally prepare himself, and he just wasn't ready. Daniel started to reminisce about his mum—her cooking, her laughter, how she was always a busybody. He remembered all the times she would be there at all his sports games, this tiny lady jumping up and down rooting for him. Daniel tried to fight back the tears, but he couldn't any longer, and just as he expected, Jeremy knocked on the door and slowly entered. His eyes widened, and he ran over to Daniel.

"Mate! What happened?" Jeremy asked in a loud whisper. Daniel had to take a few moments but couldn't get his composure, so he took his mobile and typed up what his auntie had told him.

"You wanna be left alone?" Jeremy asked. Daniel nodded his head, and for once Jeremy didn't pressure him. He clearly understood. As Jeremy headed back to his room, Jeremy's mum stood outside the door. Jeremy explained what was goin' on, and she placed her hand over her heart.

In the morning around 9:10, Daniel finally made his way to the kitchen. No surprise that Jeremy's mum had made a huge breakfast. There was no arguing, so he just grabbed a plate and started fillin' it up. And also no surprise, the gang was all there.

"I'm sorry about your mum. We have been watching the news about it for the past thirty minutes," Judy said.

"Thanks. I don't want to talk about it really. I'm trying to figure stuff out. And yes, Sabrina knows. I got a text from my auntie about an hour ago. I'm just messed up and need to focus on other stuff right now," Daniel said. He was calm but understandably irritated. The gang felt it, and although they wanted to comfort him, that would have to wait for another time. The group continued to watch the television when Jessica MacGowen interrupted the channel for an important announcement.

"I'm here at the Dunino Den where a couple came across a woman hanging from this tree. There is no identification, and right now, she is only known as Jane Doe. Local authorities have encouraged anyone that has any information regarding this tragedy, that you are to call the number at the bottom of your screen."

Judy, Latrice, and Brandon sat in shock. They had just talked with the woman.

Judy asked, "What do we do?"

"Give me a moment," Latrice replied. She walked outside and called upon the spirits, almost like a prayer. She didn't want to displease them but simultaneously wanted to guarantee Julia had peace. Judy watched Latrice from the window, waiting for her answer. After thirty minutes, Latrice came back in. Judy handed her some hot cocoa and anticipated her answer. Latrice looked sombrely at Judy, and turned to tell them, "It was interesting that when I called upon the spirits, the spirit of the east was most vocal, indicating we need to see things in a broader view and with a discerning eye. We shall make an anonymous phone call to the police to give them her name, but the rest will be up to the authorities. In this perilous time surrounding Beith, we cannae risk drawing more attention that what the dead already have." Latrice looked at the group. "I don't like it either, but this is how it is. I will use a burner mobile so our mobiles can't be traced, and I will call the authorities myself."

Then Brandon thought of an idea. "Maybe we should go there again at night and see if she left anything in her home for us."

"That's actually a brilliant idea, but now is not the time. The area could be under surveillance, but we can definitely explore that idea closer to Christmas," Latrice replied.

"Well, in the meantime, we have Winter Solstice to celebrate. We are decorating my house and sharing stories," Judy exclaimed.

None of the guys were interested in their festivities but told them to enjoy themselves. Although everyone knew they had to remain vigilant, the blissful moments were more than welcome for the time being.

Chapter 8

THE RITUALISTS

"It was nice of Siobhan and her grove to agree to come to Beith. I had a great time at your house sharing Winter Solstice with them," Latrice said.

"Me as well," Judy replied.

They shared an uneasy smile. Judy and Latrice had no idea what was coming. Then Latrice changed the subject. "I hope they can help us. Maybe the spirits spoke with Siobhan about our situation."

"I'm sure they'll bring some decent insight. We have missed out on so much since...well, you know, and we are basically starting all over again," Judy proclaimed.

Judy looked at her watch, and it was six at night right on the dot. Judy took a sip of her drink, and Latrice was nervously bouncing her legs up and down. Judy stood up and peeked around the corner to face the front door. It was then Siobhan and part of her grove appeared. Judy got their attention to come towards the back. Siobhan gave a slight smile, and she and her grove walked towards the back. Judy and Latrice greeted them, and it wasn't long before one of the ladies took their drink order.

"You remember Nimnh *(neeve)*, Eimear *(eemar)*, and Grainne *(grawna)*."

"Yes! Of course!" Judy exclaimed. Each of the ladies rendered a smile and responded with a thank you.

"Quaint little place. Kinda reminds me of An Bobhán, in Cork," Siobhan said.

"Ye, this is a popular place. Normally they have a band playin' tonight, but they cancelled because they got into an accident out on A66," Judy stated.

"Indeed. I think that's the accident we saw comin' into Beith," Grainne said.

"Well, I'm glad you made it here safe, and you don't have to worry about going back tonight. The councillor has made special accommodations for you at the inn just down the road," Latrice stated.

Raising her eyebrow in confusion, Siobhan asked, "Why would he do that?"

There was a pause.

"Let me guess. It's because he believes we can help with your possessed town?"

"To be honest, yes," Latrice replied.

Siobhan said sternly, "Look. We are not going to be here long, and we don't want to spend our holiday involved with whatever is going on here. We definitely don't want it disturbing our grove."

Judy perked up immediately. She saw the look of defeat on Latrice's face.

"We completely understand, we just wanted—" Judy started to verify, before she was cut off.

Siobhan looked at Latrice and boldly stated, "You normally have people speak for you?"

Latrice sat up a little straighter in her chair and looked sternly into Siobhan's eyes. "No one speaks for me, but I keep my grove well informed!"

"Ah. There's the high priestess. I wondered where she went," Siobhan said, before taking a sip of her drink.

"I didn't go anywhere. You just don't know about the stress and heartache we have endured," Latrice stated.

"Not fully but the spirits have given us visions of death, stealing of souls, and intimations of unsolved mysteries. Does that sum it up?" Siobhan stated.

"Pretty much," Latrice replied.

"So then, how can we help you?" Siobhan asked.

"Maybe start from the beginning," Judy suggested.

Latrice looked at Judy and sighed. She paused and told their new Irish friends about Agnes, Anna's rune, the shadow that was actually their teacher for a time, the dead, and burying the altar, meeting Julia. Everything. Latrice became exhausted just talking about it. She wanted answers, not more mysteries to solve.

"Wow! You really do need our help. You mentioned about a rune. Do you have a picture of it?" Siobhan asked.

Judy brought it up on her mobile and showed Siobhan. Siobhan's eyes widened, and she looked at her ladies. She wanted to get more information before she would explain her theory.

"What did Julia say about the rune?" Siobhan asked.

"Something about a witch needs to be involved to solidify the runes, which would put some writings on her. If not done correctly, it can bring evil, not repel it," Judy explained.

"Interesting. Since Julia is a witch, then another family member has to be a Druid. Julia was mostly correct, but it seems she was trying to protect another family member. This rune is a warning, meaning a rune warder with both abilities, witch and Druid, placed this on her. That other stuff about having writings or whatever is utter shite," Siobhan stated.

Judy and Latrice looked at each other and gave the expression of *Not again*!

"You have got to be kidding me! OK. Let's think this through. Agnes, grandparents, Thomas—they're dead. Sabrina, Anna's younger sister; Irene, her auntie; and Daniel, her brother, don't dabble with Druidism nor are practicing witches, so they're out of the picture. Who would be left?" Latrice asked. Exasperated and frustrated didn't even scratch the surface of what she was feeling.

"Maybe we are thinking about the wrong family line," Judy stated.

"In order to put such a rune on someone, they would require a particular tome and both witch and Druid abilities," Niamh said.

Latrice looked at Judy. "What do you suggest?"

"It must be someone on Julia's side of the family. Maybe we should search for her mother?" Judy suggested.

Latrice nodded and looked towards Niamh and asked, "What type of tome?"

"There is only one of its kind. The golden tome. As the name implies, it's made of gold and has the most ancient of spells that Druids should never perform single-handedly. It is more for inspiration and knowledge to help groves deal with situations like yours," Niamh said.

Latrice shook her head in disbelief and covered her face with her hands. She lifted her head and proclaimed, "We were lied to. I'm not sure which parts were true, but Julia lived in the den to protect the rune warder. I'm sure some of the things she talked about were true but really didn't apply to her."

"I guess there is nothing really to do but find the family member on Julia's side and find the golden tome," Latrice proclaimed.

Siobhan raised her beer with a smile and stated, "See, you don't need our help anyway. Cheers!"

Simultaneously, they clanged their glasses together. Siobhan looked at Latrice and gently placed her hand over Latrice's wrist.

"It's going to be OK. We have a saying in Ireland: 'Time and patience brings a snail to Cork.' It means getting to your desired goal isn't going to be smooth or fast, but time and patience are required to get to your destination," Siobhan said.

"That's fittin'," Latrice responded. She smiled and nodded to show her appreciation. Latrice had a newfound respect for Siobhan. She was truly a respected high priestess.

Latrice looked over at Judy inquisitively, wondering who she was texting.

"We have guests, Judy. What is so important?"

"Well, I'll have you know, High Priestess, I was just messaging Brandon about the golden tome. He said we need to go to Edinburgh and seek out the ritualist," Judy said with a little sarcasm.

Siobhan quickly rose from her seat and went to pay the bill. She came back to the table and said, "We need to go!"

Judy and Latrice looked at each other in bewilderment.

"You do realise you are our guests, and now we are in debt to you, right? That is the Scottish way," Latrice stated.

"You do realise there are certain things you must not mention when you are being spied on?" Siobhan retorted.

"What?!" Latrice exclaimed.

"We need to go. Now!" Siobhan stated.

They all rushed to their vehicles.

"Follow me to my house," Latrice stated.

As they drove away, there were two men in tan trench coats standing next to the front door. They didn't try to go after them but instead were seen getting on their mobiles.

When they arrived at Latrice's house, Latrice and Judy checked each of the rooms for any disturbances. Nothing seemed out of place nor damaged as if to indicate someone broke in.

"OK. We are safe. For now at least," Latrice said.

"Please. Take a seat. I'll make us some tea. I messaged Brandon to get the rest of the grove here now. Once they arrive, I'm certain you will explain what all that was about," Judy confirmed. Her tone was pleasant at first but turned sharp to indicate no more bullshit. Judy knew their new Irish friends knew more than what they were portraying.

Soon Brandon, Kristine, and Jacquelyn arrived.

"Ah, what the hell is going on? And who are these people?" Kristine asked, folding her arms, giving a smug look. Kristine would say whatever was on her mind without asking permission. If there was one person in the grove you didn't want to cross, it was her.

"Well, I know my text seemed startling but first things first. These are our guests from Ireland. Siobhan, Nimnh, Eimear, and Grianne. They are in Scotland for holiday but have also agreed to help us with our latest mystery. We were at the Gateside Inn, and when I mentioned to Latrice about what you"—she looked at Brandon—"said about the ritualists, Siobhan quickly told us to get out. Sure enough, two men in tan coats watched us drive away," Judy explained. She looked at Siobhan and continued, "Now it's your turn to explain."

It looked like a scene from Edward Bruce from the fourteenth century about to go to war to take over Ireland. For Judy, Kristine, and Jacquelyn, crossed arms and stern looks were their weapons to intimidate their so-called Irish friends. Brandon saw this and called a truce.

"Ladies, shall I play the guitar or my lute to soothe your anger? Allow our friends to speak!"

Latrice looked at Brandon in amusement. "This is the second time you have amazed me!"

Latrice looked at everyone. “He’s right! We all know that people are watching Beith and figuring out that we are starting to piece things together. I was sure once Brandon and Christian talked to the priest, and we started hearing about the ritualists, things were going to become overwrought. It is evident that word got to Edinburgh that we know about the ritualists, and they are trying to keep us at bay. That means we need to get to Edinburgh and seek out this ritualist and try to get our hands on this tome. Convince him that we need it for our scenario.”

“Exactly. Let me first apologise for scaring you. The ritualists are not ones to reckon with. They will eliminate those who bring a threat to the church. The spirits warned us of troubles that will likely be drawn to your path, which cannot be evaded. You are immune to what the ritualists will do to your grove if you investigate further,” Siobhan stated.

“We have to have faith in the spirits’ protection more than ever now. We have to do what is right for the dead that have reappeared. Give them peace. This will be the plan going forward. Since the unknown men may spend their time here in Beith watching us, Judy and I cannot go to Edinburgh. Kristine and Jacquelyn will go. No one will suspect them,” Latrice stated.

“Oh great. Send us on your suicide mission,” Kristine retorted.

“You do realise what is going on in Beith, right? You know the dead are back, and people are after us now. Does that mean anything to you?” Judy said, throwing back sarcasm.

Kristine rolled her eyes.

"Kristine and I will handle it," Jacquelyn assured her. She looked at Kristine in a way to shut her up.

"I know you will. And I hear you, Kristine. Trust in the spirits. Trust in yourself," Latrice stated. Her tone was soft, and she knew Kristine needed to hear it. Then she continued, "Brandon, maybe you and Christian can talk to the priest again and find out the best way to get a meeting with the ritualist."

"Probably not a good idea, since he is likely the one that told the ritualist about Druids inquiring about him and inevitably sent the two men we saw," Grianne stated.

"Good point. We will have to go on our own. Brandon, talk to Daniel to see if Kristine and Jacquelyn can use his house. We can assure Ms. Irene that no Druidism will be conducted inside the home," Latrice stated.

"Will do," Brandon replied.

"Ah, Latrice, I think those men found your house. There is a strange car outside with two men sitting inside using binos," Eimear said. She waved and smiled to the man using the binos. The man quickly turned on his headlights and sped off.

"They left," Eimear said.

"They'll be back for sure. We need to activate our plans now," Latrice stated.

The next day Kristine was packing and becoming angry again. She contemplated whether or not saving Beith, again, was worth all this drama. However, she quickly came back to reality and knew she and Jacquelyn had been given a huge task. Also, in order to keep the others safe, they were the ones that had to go. She took a break and looked outside. Cloudy and cold as usual. Then she noticed a strange car with two men inside. She called the police and told them two men had been following her for the past two days. Once he hung up, Kristine grabbed her coat and headed right for them. They started to pull away, but she jumped in front of the vehicle.

"Stop the car! Get out now!" Kristine demanded.

The driver stopped and got out but didn't say a word.

"Who are you, and what do you want? But I'm letting you know now that following me and being a creeper is not an option!" Kristine stated.

The man still didn't say anything.

"No worries, then. You will have to answer to them," Kristine stated. She smiled because the men were stuck. They had to tell the police the purpose for their uninvited visit.

"Are you, lass, the one that called?" the officer asked.

"Yes, and these are the weird men who have been following me. I've never seen them before in my life!" Kristine stated.

"Sir, I'm going to have to see your identification and papers for this vehicle," the officer stated.

The man took his ID from his wallet, and the passenger handed him the registration.

"Sir, I'm going to have to have you step out as well," the officer stated.

The officer in the passenger seat called for backup and stepped out to retrieve the men's information.

"So, Mr. Ruppert and Mr. Dean, you're a long way from home. Says here Edinburgh. What is the purpose of your visit?" the officer asked.

The men didn't answer. The officer's partner stepped up, and just then the backup officers arrived.

"Gents, either you answer us, or we make you answer. In other words, you don't have a choice," the officer stated.

"Our boss sent us to spy on the Druids here and see how they are handling the situation and what they know," Mr. Ruppert replied.

"Who is your boss?" the officer asked.

"We are not at liberty to say," Mr. Ruppert replied.

"Very well then," the officer said. He turned to the other officers and said, "Take Mr. Ruppert and Mr. Dean from Edinburgh to the station and impound the car."

The gentlemen were cuffed and put in the back of the second vehicle.

"Lass, never approach a strange vehicle. You could have gotten injured or killed," the officer told her.

"I understand, Officer," Kristine replied.

"When we find out more information, we will let ye know," the officer said.

"Thank you so much, Officer. I feel much safer now," Kristine said.

Kristine walked back up to her door and turned around, watching the cars drive away. She then went inside and called Latrice to tell her what happened.

"Goodness! Only you with your fortitude would be able to accomplish that. Thank the spirits you are safe! Just promise me you won't be that reckless in Edinburgh," Latrice stated.

"Sorry, High Priestess. I cannae promise that. Better hope no one sets me off!" Kristine stated.

"Kristine!" Latrice yelled. Kristine laughed. "At least you bought us some time. Well, you and Jacquelyn be safe. Ms. Irene is expecting you two, so do remember she is not a Druid and won't accept any Druid practices in her house."

Kristine and Jacquelyn arrive in Edinburgh, and the bustling city intrigued their senses. Hundreds of people walked through the castle, bagpipers and dancers performed for those circled around them, and shops lined the large cobblestone streets as far as the eye could see. The houses looked like old mystical Victorian houses that were only seen in magazines.

Kristine tried to keep her eyes on the road while actively enjoying the sights around her. She exclaimed, "We need to move here!"

They drove by the University of Edinburgh, and Kristine almost swerved off the road eyeing the striking university men in their proper navy-blue suits, jackets, and scarves that warmed their necks. Kristine couldn't contain herself. "Oh yeah! We are definitely moving here!"

"Well, before we move, pay attention to the road, please. I would like to get to Ms. Irene's house in one piece," Jacquelyn said.

Kristine rolled her eyes.

"We will come back for sure, but remember, we have our mission that needs attending," she said.

Kristine rolled her eyes again and went back to the more important topic—Edinburgh.

"All I have to say is two years, then we'll be here. Roommates, we'll have the hottest partners on campus, the professors will love us! I have this all planned!"

Laurie pondered the notion of not coming to Edinburgh just to hear Kristine's reaction.

"What if I wanted to go to college in London?"

Kristine made a gruesome face and responded, "I don't appreciate you speaking rubbish in my vehicle. Go vomit that glaikit nonsense somewhere else please!"

"OK. Clearly not going to London then." Jacquelyn laughed.

Sabrina constantly anticipated their arrival by looking out the window, moving the dark green curtains back, then closing them again.

"They'll be here soon enough, Sabrina!" Irene stated. She was fussing about in the kitchen, ensuring the haggis was cooking properly and that snacks and drinks were available, then tidying a bit in the sitting room. Sabrina turned around for her twentieth time, checking for Daniel's friends, and watched her auntie buzzing around.

Watching her reminded Sabrina of her mother doing the same thing. She didn't dare say it, but she enjoyed seeing a part of her mum within her auntie.

Irene looked at Sabrina curiously. "What are you smiling at?"

"Oh, nothing!" Sabrina said, grinning even more from ear to ear.

Irene stopped, sighed, and realised what Sabrina was grinning about.

"Let me guess. I fuss like your mother did."

"Yep!" Sabrina giggled.

"Well, I guess we picked that up from your grandmother. Her house was always immaculate and ready to welcome guests," Irene replied. She suspected that Sabrina was hesitant to mention her mother in front of her. It was time for Irene to put aside her own feelings for her sister and allow Sabrina to share whatever was really bothering her.

Irene stopped her fussing for a moment, sat on the couch, and motioned for Sabrina to sit next to her. "Come here, child."

Sabrina was a wee apprehensive because her auntie was looking a bit serious.

"For a long time, I have been trying to keep you and Daniel safe from the limelight due to your mother's transgressions. I believe I sent the wrong message implying you can't speak of her, which is incorrect. People grieve differently, and if you ever want to talk about her or to vent, let me know. I'm here for you." She grabbed Sabrina and held her tight.

"Auntie, can I be honest about something?" Sabrina asked.

"Of course, love," Irene replied.

"I'm actually more upset with Anna than Mum. I mean, I know my mum caused a lot of pain, and I believe her punishment is justified. I'm not daft, but Anna shouldn't have been so inquisitive to look outside. She knew better, and in my eyes, she was selfish!" Sabrina stated.

Irene was a little taken aback and wasn't sure how to respond. She had to use her words carefully because she wanted to keep her trust.

"Well, I did not expect that point of view, although it's understandable. You probably don't know every detail of your mother's involvement, which is why you feel like you do."

Irene was still holding Sabrina and softly moving her hand down her hair. Irene wasn't sure who needed more comfort, her or Sabrina. Then Sabrina continued expressing more of her shocking thoughts.

"I mean, I could have my father here at least if it weren't for Anna. I know she's at the centre, but I have no desire to see her!" Sabrina stated. Her words were profound and full of mixed emotions because she loved and admired Anna. Hearing this hurt Irene's heart, and Irene hoped in time Sabrina would forgive Anna.

"I understand your anger, but allow me to put it in this perspective: your sister is dead. Bless her, of course, but haven't we all been known to make mistakes we regret? There comes a time in our lives where we just need to let go because it's the past. Grudges only hurt us. Do you understand, love?"

"I guess. So are you mad at me?" Sabrina asked, trying to stop greetin' a bit. Sabrina's face was flushed with worry because she didn't want to disappoint her. Irene smiled and moved her hair from her face.

"Of course I am! How dare you say such things!" Irene laughed, joking with Sabrina.

"Oh my gosh, Auntie! Don't scare me like that!" Sabrina yelled. They both laughed.

Sabrina went back to the window, drawing the curtains to view the street. Irene thought that maybe in time she'd tell Sabrina everything or never say a word more about it. Sabrina's points were valid based on the knowledge she had. For now, Irene left it at that.

Sabrina saw a white car pull up in the driveway and jumped up and down.

"They're here!"

"Go see if they need help with their luggage," Irene said.

As Sabrina opened the door, there stood Rebecca.

"So is that them?" Rebecca asked.

"Yep! Come on!" Sabrina said. She snagged Rebecca by the arm and pulled her to the car.

"Hey! I'm Kristine, and this is Jacquelyn." She looked at Sabrina and said, "You are so adorable! Just like we were at that age."

Jacquelyn replied with her typical sarcasm, "Yeah. Four years was so long ago. She's almost a teenager. You do realise that, right?"

"This is my best mate, Rebecca. She's really here for my auntie's cookin'," Sabrina said.

Rebecca reciprocated the sarcasm. "Pretty much. Sabrina is boring." She looked at Sabrina, and said, "Kidding."

Kristine looked at Jacquelyn and said, "We're definitely going to get along!"

Sabrina went to grab Kristine's bag, but Kristine told her thank you but that she'd take it.

Once they came across the threshold, Kristine and Jacquelyn felt uneasy. They couldn't pinpoint it right away. Maybe because there were no Druids present or it was just odd being in a stranger's home. Irene came from the kitchen and asked them to please sit down.

"Hello and welcome. Daniel expressed that your Druid mission is vital to the release of the dead. I'm certain you can't give me particulars, but I do want to confirm that no Druidism chants, prayers, et cetera, are welcome here. This is very much a Christian home, and well, anything else is not part of our beliefs. I hope you understand."

"Yes, Ms. Irene. Our mission actually doesn't involve any of that. But to keep you safe and our mission safe, we cannot tell you anything more as to why we are in Edinburgh," Jacquelyn stated.

"That's fine by me. Since young Rebecca has not had proper haggis, I'm makin' that with tatties for supper. Normally, I would make it for Burns Night, but I felt like this was a special occasion. It should be ready in a few hours. In the meantime, Sabrina will show you where all the snacks are. Tomorrow I'm ordering a bunch of chippy boxes."

Kristine and Jacquelyn had confused looks on their faces, as though they were visiting another country.

"Forgive me, but what are chippy boxes?" Kristine asked.

Sabrina immediately and excitedly answered, "They are fried everything! Pizza, chicken, onion rings. You name it. It's the worst thing for ye, but it tastes so good!"

Kristine and Jacquelyn looked at each other with amazement. Kristine replied, "We would love that!"

"Then it's settled. Sabrina will show you to your rooms, and I'll call you when supper is ready," Irene said.

Irene smiled while drying some dishes. She was happy for Sabrina, and Daniel assured her that the young ladies would be nice to her. It had been a very long time since so many people were in her house. The only time she saw people was when she went to her coffee shop and checked up on her employees and helped with inventory. Outside of that, it was peaceful. Putting dishes in the cupboard, Irene heard them laughing.

Once Kristine and Jacquelyn settled in their room, Kristine wanted to talk about tomorrow. They had to talk quietly so Ms. Irene didn't think they were disrespecting her rules.

"So tomorrow we have our appointment with you know who, and we are to say what exactly?"

"Basically what does he know about Beith, and how he can help free the dead or get their spirits back?" Jacquelyn said. She noticed Kristine looking uncertain and wanted to reassure her that everything would be fine. "Don't worry. Let me do most of the talking, and if needed, you strongly reiterate that we need answers, like you would do when someone upsets you. You know, your normal."

Kristine smiled a little cunningly and said, "I can do that."

They went to Sabrina's room and knocked on the door. Sabrina welcomed them, and Kristine and Jacquelyn looked around unsure what they had just walked into. Rebecca saw their facial expressions and right away said, "Creepy, right? I know."

"Is this a shrine or something?" Kristine asked. Jacquelyn was wondering the same thing with all the crosses on each wall. Sabrina didn't take it to heart. She thought their expressions were funny.

"My auntie just wants me safe in all aspects."

"Clearly," Kristine responded. To get the ick feeling off her, she changed the subject.

"So what are you all doin'?"

"Oh, just hiding this Druid book from Ms. Irene," Rebecca stated. Kristine and Jacquelyn went into shock. Kristine had to see what they were talking about first before calling Latrice.

"Right. Let me see it, please," Kristine stated. She didn't want to sound too demanding, but it was imperative that she see it.

"Rebecca, you promised!" Sabrina said. She was exasperated and upset that Rebecca would even say anything. Rebecca quickly tried to reason with her.

"They're Druids. It could be essentially their book anyway."

"I know, but that is the only type of book that reminds me of my mum," Sabrina replied.

Kristine tried not to let her nonverbals show, but it was difficult. She instantly thought, *Does this wee yin have a clue on what her mum did?* Sabrina dubiously handed the white book over to Kristine. Kristine removed the brown paper protecting the cover and couldn't believe her eyes. Could this be the tome they were looking for?

"Where did you find this?!"

"At my school's library. The school librarian knows I have it, but she gave it to me. Meaning, I never have to check it back in. It's kinda like we have a mutual understanding," Sabrina said.

Kristine pulled out her mobile and snapped pictures and sent them to Latrice. Kristine's mobile instantly rang. It was Latrice.

"I thought Sabrina was a Christian?"

"Trust me. Jesus is everywhere, and I mean everywhere here. She said she got this from her school library. Is this the golden tome? It does have gold on it," Kristine said.

"Unfortunately not. We are looking for a pure gold tome. Something very sacred, hence why the both of you are there," Latrice stated.

"Right. Tomorrow is when we go," Kristine replied.

"Keep me updated, and bring back that white book, please. That might have to be properly burned as well. Thank you and be safe," Latrice said.

"What did she say?" Jacquelyn asked.

Sabrina wasn't going to like Kristine's answer, but it was best for everyone's safety.

"We're taking the book with us. You didn't do any spells from this book or anything like that, did you?"

Sabrina frowned and wanted the book back but knew she had to relinquish it into proper hands. She felt they were taking the one thing she had of her mum. "I read it but not like out loud or whatever. I just wanted to read the books my mum read."

Kristine wanted to be truthful and very matter of fact. Jacquelyn saw it in her face but stopped her from saying anything.

"Kristine. Don't!"

Kristine wanted to tell her that her mum was the lady of destruction and only used the black book for her bidding. Sabrina saw her look angry at the situation and wanted to know what she knew.

"It's OK. You can tell me."

"Our high priestess wouldn't approve of such conversation. I think it would be best if your auntie told you," Jacquelyn intervened. She added, "I think our journey was overstimulating for us. On the way here, we saw these hot guys, the castle, so many shops. We are just hungry and want to go to bed."

Jacquelyn did her best to lighten the mood. Kristine and Jacquelyn realised that the uneasy feeling they initially sensed wasn't from all the crosses; it was from the book's presence.

Irene yelled from the other room that dinner was ready. The girls exchanged hugs while ensuring Sabrina's well-being.

The next day, Kristine and Jacquelyn quietly ate their breakfast. Both of them couldn't stop thinking about the white book, Sabrina thinking her mum was all grand, and meeting the ritualist today. Jacquelyn looked at Kristine. Her make-up was perfect as usual, but she still looked like she hadn't slept in days.

"You OK?"

"Ye. I think we're thinking about the same things. I do want to make sure we get the you-know-what in the boot before we head out today," Kristine replied.

"That won't be an issue. It's already been done," Jacquelyn assured.

"See? This is why we are best mates!" Kristine said. They both laughed softly.

Once they completed their meal, they freshened up and left for St. Kirks Cathedral.

When they arrived, they couldn't very well just walk in and ask for the ritualist. They had to be a little more imaginative. A lady caretaker approached them and smiled. The elderly woman, with a medium build, stood 162 centimetres and had black hair with grey strands pinned in a bun.

"Welcome, lasses. How may I help you?"

"Hello. We would like to see someone that has knowledge of Scotland's archives," Jacquelyn said.

The caretaker looked at them incongruously.

"It's for our thesis to get into the university," Kristine stated. She kept eye contact with the caretaker until she broke her silence again.

"Very well. This way. Please keep silent as we walk to the back. Many are studying or preparing sermons."

The girls agreed and followed the woman down the long corridor. Each couple of steps there was mini archway embedded in the wall symbolizing a particular saint or martyred priest. They got to the end where one door stood. The woman pulled out a large grouping of keys that clanged as she tried to find the correct key. She unlocked it, and they walked a short distance until they reached a hidden elevator, which needed another key to activate it. Soon the door screeched open, and the noise made it sound as if it hadn't been oiled for decades. The woman directed the ladies to go in first, then she stepped in, used another key to make the elevator door close, and headed down.

Kristine and Jacquelyn didn't feel like they were right for this mission. They held each other's hand tight until blood flow ceased in their fingers. This didn't seem normal at all. They reached the bottom floor, and the elevator opened. The caretaker looked at them and said,

"This way."

The girls saw another woman standing next to a large executive desk made of the finest oak.

"Thank you, Madam Caretaker. I'll take it from here," the woman said.

They watched as the elevator door closed. The dim lights in the large grey room did not ease their fears. The woman before them stood 170 centimetres, had her auburn hair pinned in a bun, was slender, had bright-blue eyes, and was dressed in a black skirt, a red blouse, and a black jacket. The woman decided to get the formalities out of the way.

"Hello and welcome to the archives. I am Samantha, caretaker of all and any information about Scotland and the keeper for the ritualist. I can presume you are not here for a school project." She smiled.

"You would presume correctly. We are here—" Jacquelyn started before being interrupted by Samantha.

"I know why you are here. Father Mac called anticipating your arrival and said that you may want to see the ritualist. However, you must inform me of the importance first before I allow you entry."

Jacquelyn took a deep breath and told her exactly what the high priestess told her to say if the situation became problematic.

"Of no disrespect, but our high priestess informed us to only talk to the ritualist, and I cannae disobey her as a vowed ovate."

"Well, I'm sorry, lasses, but you won't see him today," Samantha stated.

Kristine figured that was her cue to arbitrate the matter. She looked over towards the long corridor that presumably led to the ritualist and noticed the two men who were outside her house.

"Ah, Samantha. It's not like the ritualist is the great and powerful Oz. He's a high-end priest who keeps tabs on other religions so they don't interfere with yours. Have you seen the news? Beith is in a world of shite, and we need his help. On top of that, those two swines over there were spying on our grove to see what we knew about you. So we are not taking no for an answer. Is that now good enough for you?"

Jacquelyn didn't say a word and stood there as though to say *You had it comin', lady!*

Samantha was impressed by the Druid's fortitude and absolute loyalty to their high priestess.

"You have proven yourself worthy. Wait here."

Jacquelyn and Kristine gave each other a look of uncertainty as Samantha left them mentally disarrayed. Kristine stared at the two men by the corridor entryway and silently mouthed *mongo* and flipped them the bird. Jacquelyn whispered to her to stop. Just when Kristine put her hands down, Samantha came around the corner.

"They're harmless really. They were just doing what I asked them to."

Samantha held in her hand a book wrapped in yellow cloth with a light-yellow ribbon to make it look like a gift. She passed the book over to Kristine.

"Are you the ritualist?"

"No, he's back there, but what you need is in your hands now. When the book wishes to be seen, it will show itself. You are now the keeper of the golden tome, and the only way to read it is to use humility, compassion, and love," Samantha instructed.

"Can I ask a favour, please?" Kristine asked. Samantha grinned as she read her thoughts.

"Yes, I will keep these two away from Beith, and yes, I will advise the ritualist Beith poses no danger to the Catholic Church."

"Wow! You're good," Kristine stated.

"Madam Caretaker will see you to the cathedral's entrance. I'm sure we'll see each other again soon. Be safe, lassies," Samantha said. She watched as the door of the elevator closed and put all her hope in the arms of the young Druid. She had interfered once and failed. Hopefully, this grove could free her family.

Chapter 9

THE NETHERWORLD

Nixia made her way to her earthly home. The netherworld was wonderful, but she would rather be standing in her luxurious furnished detached home. It had everything she wanted. She lived on the top floor, which meant each spacious bedroom had a curved ceiling with a large skylight. The newly renovated kitchen had light wooden cabinets with navy-blue marble countertops, an oven, a dishwasher, and a washing machine that did both washing and drying cycles. She absolutely loved the bathroom, which had a stylish four-piece suite—triple-sized bathtub, separate shower, heated toilet, and double sink. Her favourite part was the entrance hallway leading to the upper landing. The large area could entertain many people, and the best part was looking down upon the city. Especially at night. The lights, the traffic, and the people bustling about—there was a part of Nixia that envied the humans and their freedom to choose their way of life and not live in fear of eternal death. Particularly if they did something unfavourable. Nixia couldn't tell her father, the dark king, no less, to piss off. That certainly would not be in her best interest. For now, she would revel in her earthly domain.

After binging on the finest wines and being catered to by the best chef in Edinburgh, Nixia woke up the next morning feeling refreshed. She needed to the take the day to familiarize herself with Edinburgh, the cathedral, and how she would enter the archives. The caretakers could see past her façade, which complicated things. Nixia had to ensure she didn't use her demon powers or cause much blood to spill to attract attention. Hopefully, she could enter using just her charm.

Of course, she couldn't go around town with a sharp, slashing tail and jagged teeth, so Nixia shape-shifted herself. With a quick snap of her fingers, she had long, black wavy hair, deep-green eyes, perfect white human teeth, and definitely no tail. She wore a peach-coloured Celtic sweater, black tights, and high chocolate-coloured boots. Of course, she already had the body of a young supermodel that would make men turn their heads and slide their sunglasses down for a clearer look.

She donned her long black wool coat, black thick-knitted hat, and red scarf and headed into town. Although she had her own vehicle and driver, now wasn't the time to show off. Nixia didn't need to bring any extra attention to herself.

Walking by a row of books, Samantha caressed the shelf where the golden book once sat. She knew Kristine would care for it well but feared a demon from the netherworld would soon come and attempt to claim it. As she walked farther along, flashes of visions came to her. Just as she suspected, pictures of the cathedral, the golden book, the streets leading up to the cathedral, and demons occupied her mind. When the visions stopped, she leisurely walked to her desk and picked up the phone.

"Madam Caretaker, could you please come see me at your earliest convenience?"

The woman on the other end agreed. She knew "earliest convenience" meant now. While Samantha was the keeper of the ritualist and an Arch Druid, she didn't aggrandize her status. She was genuinely humble, wise, and had solid intuition, hence why she needed to alert the caretaker of her visions.

A few moments later, the elevator doors squeaked open. Samantha loathed every time they would open because it sounded like a banshee had her wings caught in the door.

Before Samantha talked with the caretaker, she gave the two guards the task of oiling every hinge of the door.

"The oil is on the top floor in the supply closet, gentlemen."

"Yes, Keeper!" one guard stated. He did a slight bow, and both guards departed.

"I don't know how you have dealt with those doors for so long, Madam Caretaker!" Samanta said.

"I'm certain you didn't call me here to discuss elevator doors," Madam Caretaker suggested.

Samantha felt it was her way to make small talk, but clearly the caretaker wasn't in the mood for mundane pleasantries.

"Right. Please be aware demons have arrived in Edinburgh. My visions tell me that they are near and coming to the cathedral. If you have any suspicions about anyone, reject them!"

There were footsteps coming from the long corridor behind them. The footsteps had a steady gait and seemed to get faster as the sound got closer. Both ladies turned around and were surprised to see Father David.

"Ritualist! A pleasant surprise indeed. I did not hear my phone ring."

"Well, I would hope not, considering I didn't call," Father David replied. They shared a chuckle. Father David was very devoted to the church, his faith, and all the community's safety. It was paramount that he would be kept informed of all matters that could potentially be a detriment to the church. He then inquired about Beith and other matters.

"I heard the word demon. What news do you have on Beith?"

Samantha turned to the caretaker and said, "Thank you for your assistance, that will be all."

Samantha heard the elevator start its descent and knew the two guards would appear momentarily. Just as Madam Caretaker turned to face the elevator, the doors opened. No sound.

"Gentlemen, excellent work. Thank you!"

The guards started walking back to their post and noticed Father David.

"Is everything all right, Father?" one gentleman asked.

Father David assured both guards that everything was well. He even told them to take the rest of the day off. The men looked puzzled as if it were a test of their loyalty, so they stayed at their post. However, Father David insisted and said that their loyalty had been proven worthy. Samantha was perplexed by his willingness to excuse the guards. Normally they would have to be there no matter the cost.

"That was very generous of you."

Father David enjoyed watching Samantha try to decipher his motives. Then he said, "Please. Update me on Beith."

She knew he didn't like anything to do with Druids or other religions, but she had to tell him what she saw.

"Ritualist. I don't necessarily have news directly on Beith, but indirectly, one of the Druids from there came here, and I gave her the golden tome. I gave them instructions on how to use it, but I hope the young girl remembers how in their time of need. Secondly, my visions were quite clear today. Demons are present in Edinburgh, and they are coming here. I suspect in the next day or so."

Father David looked at her attentively. He saw the concern in her eyes.

"What else do you know about tomes and other books involving Beith?"

She wasn't sure where Father David was going with his inquiries, but she became worried for the grove in Beith. As keeper, she had to tell him whatever he wanted to know at any given time. For the first time, she was hesitant to reveal anything to him.

"Ritualist. There is a black book known for its demonic, witch-casting spells. There is its opposite, the white book, that good witches would use for chanting the corners, spells of the earth, and healing. The golden tome only reveals itself to those that have humility, compassion, and love. If one of the characteristics is missing, then it will not reaveal its powerful spells. It's not demonic. Its power overrides any Druid book."

Father David stood there for a moment and then replied, "We should have helped them long before now. I don't approve of your religion, nor will I ever understand it; however, whatever you can do to help those in Beith, do so."

He turned around and headed back to chamber. Samantha stood in shock. This was her first recollection of him taking interest in another religion's well-being. She did not get the impression that there was anything sinister behind his words. It was likely he understood that not all other religions were wicked, and it didn't require them to be part of their beliefs but coexist in respect for one another. A feat the ritualist seemed to master today.

The partly clouded, chilly day welcomed many visitors to the cathedral. This would be the last weekend for public tours before they resumed next year. People from all over the world came to marvel at the history and architecture of the First Presbyterian Church. From a majority Catholic Scotland, ruled by Mary, Queen of Scots, the Scottish Parliament had ruled for removal of papal rule, which led Scotland into Presbyterianism. Since then, the cathedral had survived civil wars, renovations, and additions, such as including a stained-glassed window shrine representing Robbie Burns.

Samantha arrived early to the cathedral that day. She felt that the malicious spirit was close and that she needed to put a protection spell over the ritualist's corridor. Samantha thought that if the demon could possibly get through the crowds and get to the archives undetected, it meant two things: one, it was likely a high-ranking demon, and two, Samantha had to pull out all the stops to keep the ritualist and the archives safe.

Nixia was more than excited to find the tome. She had read online that the cathedral was having open tours and thought this was the best opportunity to get into the archives. She wasn't sure how much protection covered the cathedral, but she wasn't taking any chances. She was only going to use her powers to get where she needed to be. Nixia researched the cathedral and its history in case she was asked questions. She presumed the archives would be protected by some heavenly spiritual being or a powerful white witch. Either way, it was critical she handled everything perfectly.

As Nixia arrived at the Romanesque-style cathedral, she shed her scarf, hat, and coat and was warmly greeted by the caretaker.

"That will be £15 please, lass."

Nixia dug through her purse and pulled out a £20 note. The caretaker politely asked, "What are you most interested in seeing?"

Nixia smiled and rendered a false erudite reply. "I am interested in the shrine for Robbie Burns, the Thistle room, the library of old Bibles or something like that when Mary, Queen of Scots was here, and the architecture. This church is actually Romanesque, whereas many are structured more of the Gothic period."

The caretaker was impressed by her knowledge and enthusiasm. She handed Nixia her £5 change and gave her a pass to wear around her neck. They exchanged a smile, and the caretaker directed her to the next station.

Nixia noticed she didn't respond about the books but was otherwise impressed by her. Nixia was part of group five for the tour. Being nice and mingling was not Nixia's forte, as she was not fond of mingling with the living. However, her reward would come when she got back to her earthly home and had all the spoils she wanted. Not to mention returning to her normal self.

The group Nixia was in was a lively bunch, which made it that much more painful for her. However, she would chime in from time to time, just to fit in. They got to the chapel, and many wooden carvings of angels, flowers, and animals surrounded the area. Overseeing the carvings was a statue of St. Andrew. Nixia stood and looked at the art, while others in her group gave mere glances. Nixia was feeling something she hadn't before and wasn't sure what it was or how to explain it. She knew it was something she couldn't get from the dark king nor her mother, but when looking at St. Andrew protecting the animals, she could tell it was out of love, not fear. Fear was all Nixia knew. The sad part was that tomorrow she would have to report to her father about the tome and never hear anything loving like the carvings in the chapel seen every day.

The group now was walking sluggishly down a walkway towards the back, and Nixia noticed there was only one door. *This has to be it*, she thought. She looked around to see if anyone was watching her, and when she was right next to the locked door, she vanished into the next room. To the left were shelves of books stacked behind a U-shaped sitting area. Another room past the sitting area was a supply closet. To the right was an old tube-shaped elevator decorated on top with Gothic images in pewter. Nixia had found her golden ticket.

She noticed it required a key to enter. She placed her hand over the keyhole, and the door opened. Nixia did the same for the other keyhole from the inside, and the same when she reached the bottom. Nixia walked out and was immediately approached by Samantha. Samantha knew this was a demon in disguise.

"Looks like you lost your way."

Nixia smirked. "I don't think so." She waved her hand and knocked Samantha back a few steps.

Samantha attempted to throw a fire ball at Nixia, but Nixia absorbed it.

"It's quite simple, Druid. Give me the tome and I'll be on my way," Nixia said.

"The tome isn't here!" Samantha stated.

Nixia walked, looking at the books and tapping her long sharp claws along the book's bindings. Her eyes went from green to pure red to scan the rows of books. She realised the Druid was speaking the truth.

"Where is it? Tell me and I'll let you live."

Samantha laughed. "You can't kill me, demon, and you know that as well as I do."

Nixia walked up to her and showed Samantha her red eyes. "You gave the tome to those Druid brats in Beith. Looks like I have another place to visit."

Nixia vanished to just outside the cathedral. She couldn't stop her eyes from being red and so she put her sunglasses on. As she started to walk back to her earthly villa, she lured men to walk back with her, like a black widow waiting to eat her trapped prey.

The next day, Nixia was drinking the rest of the wine and started to kick the men out. They were no longer in a daze and wondered where they were and who she was. Like a vampire, she would drink some of their blood as though she was performing a ritual. She walked up to them with a grin, holding her goblet of wine and simultaneously showing her jagged teeth, and black eyes, and growled at them. They screamed like little girls and ran out as fast as they could. Nixia knew whatever story they told, their mates would tell them they were crazy.

Nixia snapped her fingers, and the whole house was spotless. She knew she had to leave and head to Beith to get the tome. She had to act quickly, because soon the dark king would call for her. She wasn't allowed to stay on earth for too long because she would become accustomed to human life, which wasn't fitting for a demon.

The driver was waiting for her. Nixia ensured nothing was out of place before she left and headed towards the car. He opened the door of a classic 1995 Buick Roadmaster that was customised with black leather and cloth seats in the back, black gloss exterior, and an upgrade as a glider.

She told her driver, Damien, they were heading to Beith. He looked at her from his rearview mirror and said, "Yes, Princess."

When the vehicle got to the Glasgow city limits, they were ported back to the netherworld. It was only Nixia standing in front of the dark king.

"I see you had fun, but did you get the book?"

Nixia gave a disparaging look, and frankly told the dark king, "Had I not been zapped back here and able to get to Beith, you would have had your tome!"

The dark king walked up to her and backhanded her across the face.

"How dare you talk to me that way! And you wonder why I don't allow you to stay on earth too long! You will be punished for your treachery!"

Nixia fought back like a defiant teenager and yelled, "Treachery? I'm your daughter! I have done everything for you. Worshipped the fire you walk on, and you think

I'm disloyal? It has nothing to do with spending two days on earth. I can be there as long as I want to, but to honour you, I come back. Or you bring me back. Although your plans are perfect, sometimes, other things get in the way that are out of my control. Like the Druid brats having the black book and now the golden tome!"

The dark king looked at her in disgust. He turned into the most repugnant, scariest, darkest demon. A side of him Nixia had never seen. His voice changed, which mimicked an echoing growl.

"You have defied me for the last time!"

Nixia cowered to the floor, and then he continued in his normal voice. "If you can find out who the warder is, then I will be more lenient with your punishment."

Nixia stood up, and the dark king waved the curtains opened. On one of the pods were Anna and Julia. Having the two of them there, Nixia already concluded who the warder was but wasn't going to divulge the name. In her mind, she wouldn't be able to get her either, and she would have an even bigger punishment. This was her eternal life that she didn't ask for. She knew her father would be watching, so she decided to put on a beguiling show.

The anger Nixia had towards her father was going to be directed towards Julia and Anna. She swayed as she paced backed and forth between the mother-daughter duo and couldn't wait to torture them. Her tongue danced like a snake as though she was tasting their fear.

"Well, well, well. Quite the family reunion we have here! Aren't you happy to see your mum, Anna?" she asked.

"This is not my mum, you evil witch!" Anna yelled.

"Oh." Nixia giggled and looked at Julia. "She doesn't know." Looking back at Anna, she said, "And my, aren't you feisty? By the way, I'm a demon not a witch. You can yell all you want to, but no one will hear you nor listen, because this is *my* dominion. So it is best you just keep silent. Unless you're tortured, or as I like to call it, playtime. Your little outburst will cost you some lashings!" Nixia's face turned from condescending to pure evil. She took her tail and started lashing it across Anna's face and body. The tip of her jagged tail ripped off layers of her skin.

"Enough, Nixia!" the dark king yelled. Nixia cowered before her father and backed away. "Rise, my daughter. Your time to torture may be sooner than expected."

Nixia watched as her father waved his hand over Anna, healing her face. The dark king brought Nixia closer to him and caressed her face.

"I will give you this gift in the meantime, my princess."

Nixia was surprised by her father's gesture after he recently threatened punishment. She thought, *Or was this part of his plan to fool me*?

Julia and Anna were each chained to the ground on a floating pod on fire. The pod turned to face the other, and simultaneously the doors of each pod opened. Anna saw her mother and yelled out to her trying to break out of her chains. Agnes was the mother she had known all her life. Even though Agnes had committed the ultimate betrayal against her, Anna still loved her.

"This should settle your fix for torture, my dear. Have your fun," the dark king said. He turned to walk away and then vanished.

Deviously, Nixia almost fell in love with the idea of torturing Agnes. It brought her great pleasure.

"What to do. Should I just have the nether hounds rip her to shreds? Or shall I use my tail and claws to produce the same effect? Decisions, decisions," Nixia said. She tapped her finger on her cheek. She smiled. "Hmm, why not both! Release the hounds!" Nixia yelled.

Just then, a purple portal opened where Agnes was sitting, and two nether hounds appeared.

"Devour her legs. I'll get the rest." Nixia laughed.

Anna and Julia watched in horror as they witnessed Agnes's suffering. Her anguished screams pierced their ears. Agnes fervently tried to escape, but her efforts were void. That made Nixia laugh even more. Nixia teleported herself instantly to the pod and petted the hounds as if they were her favourite pets in the world. She looked at them, and said, "Mummy's turn."

The hounds disappeared into the portal, and Nixia commenced torturing Agnes. You could hear the ripping of flesh as her tail whipped across her face. Anna would scream for Nixia to stop, but her screams fell on deaf ears. Nixia wanted to show Anna and Julia that people were not safe from Nixia's torment. Although Agnes's body was recently buried, Nixia had the power to take the body and toy with it. Just as long as she returned it.

When Nixia was finished, the floor of the pod opened, and Agnes's spirit fell into a lake of fire, while her tortured body was returned to the grave. If a graverobber were to dig up her grave, he would have found maggots eating her torn flesh.

Nixia teleported back to where Anna sat in shock. Julia not so much.

"Now it's story time." Nixia licked and swallowed the flesh from under her claws, looking at Anna. She sat down next to them as though they were friends sharing deep and dark secrets. "You see, Anna, you are Julia's daughter. Julia was raped horribly and conceived you. Because Julia couldn't take the fact of how she got pregnant, she gave you up to Agnes. The only person that knew about this arrangement was Thomas. Your father. Well, uncle really, but we'll say father. Anyway, you came from a family of witches and Druids that were not good at keeping their promises to the dark king. My wonderful father, of course. For generations, since you came into the picture, family have tried to protect you. However, the web my father weaves is pure genius, and evil tends to find its way to where it needs to go."

Anna sobbed. "What promises?"

"Excellent question. Glad you asked. It's funny really. A witch making a promise to bring souls to my father but trying to find ways to avert it. Or best yet, wanting all the power on earth and thinking it would keep them from evil. Therefore, making themselves 'a nicer witch' by proclaiming themself a Druid also. So because of these mistakes made by your true family members, a punishment had to be proclaimed. Hence the curse over your small, mundane town of Beith," Nixia said.

"Why won't you let our spirits free then?" Julia asked.

"Another great question. Well, once we find the one who put the warning rune on Anna, then we can eliminate and punish the bloodline that initially made an oath to my father. And I do remember when Anna was down here the first time we talked about her mother. Well, Julia. We have you. Now we need the rune warder. Your mother," Nixia said.

"She's dead!" Julia exclaimed.

"Nice try. I will give you time to think about that outburst, and when I decide to come back, whenever that is, I'm going to want the truth. OK? Nice talk, ladies." Nixia vanished.

The pod turned at a very slow pace, showing all the dead faces tortured within the netherworld. They listened in fear as the dead spirits wailed, cried, and screamed, which echoed throughout, and never stopped.

Julia wanted to direct the attention away from all the pain Anna was clearly suffering. "My sweet Anna. You have suffered so much."

"Was it true what the demon said? About, you know, how you conceived me?" Anna asked.

"Yes," Julia replied.

"I'm sorry that happened. And I'm not mad that you gave me up. It's understandable considering the circumstances." Anna paused and displayed a confused look. "What got you down here?" Anna asked.

"After I found out through your friends what your mother had done, I put a curse on your mother and killed her. I had no remorse. But I also broke a promise to myself to never curse someone after I cursed your real father. When I did so, it caused not only his death but the death of many innocents. Because of the curse on your mum, I hanged myself," Julia said. She didn't look sad or disappointed, but there was clearly a void. Julia knew she couldn't escape what she had done, so she sat and accepted her punishment.

"I see. I guess we have our own way to face our evils," Anna replied.

"I would like to know about you, if that's all right." Julia said. She hoped to establish something before they met their permanent fates. Anna smiled and agreed. Although the wailing in the background like a Caoineag (coin-yik) never subsided, they were able to listen to each other and drown out the misery that surrounded them.

Chapter 10

HISTORY IN THE MAKING

The air was thick on this cloudy Sunday morning. The fog kept the eerie scenery from the night before, while a slight breeze swayed the trees along the road. It wasn't long before the fog lifted and allowed rays from the sun to radiate along the ground.

The weather wasn't going to be a hindrance this day. William and his parents were busy getting the house ready for their Christmas party—their first one in over ten years. William's parents were surprised that, in light of Anna's death, he would suggest a party but decided to go all out for him.

Outside the house, multicoloured lights outlined the whole front of the house. The trees had white lights that touched every branch. Candy canes lined their long driveway, and there was a small projector that showed snowflakes upon the house. The entrance where the pillars stood had green garland with red bows, and the door had a wreath that mirrored the pillar garland. The inside was just as beautiful. William's mum just finished making sugar cookies and had cider with oranges and cloves simmering on the stove. Each window was frosted and adorned with different-coloured stained-glass snowflake ornaments. Each table had a glass lantern shaped like a Victorian house sitting on a stone base dusted with artificial snow. The windowsills were lined with frosted garland with red, white, and green bulbs, and other Christmas-themed knick-knacks filled the house. And of course, mistletoe hung from every door.

For the finale, the tree. The tree stood seven feet tall. It was as tall as it was wide. A white angel with wings glowed at the top, while the rest of the tree was decorated with purple and gold bulbs and lights. It was tradition each year to do a different theme. This year, William's mother picked out the colours. Many presents embellished under the tree. Their cat, Sunset, could be found under the tree either sleeping or batting at the bows on the presents.

William wanted to surprise his friends as well. After all, they deserved as much of a Christmas and peace for all they had done for Beith.

Since the time he refused to play a role in the curse-slaying crusade, he had time to reflect on what was important. Himself. He put off going to college so he could be with Anna, but that certainly changed. When his friends arrived, he would have more than just presents waiting for them.

"William! Could you come here, please?" William's mum shouted out. He rushed to the kitchen.

“What time are your friends coming?” she asked.

“Around 11 in the morn. Why?” William asked.

“Just wanted to make sure everything is set and ready. Do you think we are missing anything?” she asked.

“Goodness, woman! We don’t need anything else!” William’s dad yelled from across the room.

“Wheesht! I wasn’t talkin’ to you!” she said.

This was the common banter in the house that would always make William laugh. William wanted to add to the banter and spoke just a little loudly for his dad to hear. “Gee, Mum. I was wondering when you were goin’ to decorate more in the family room. It looks a little bare.”

“Shut it, boy! Yer goin’ to get your mum in a frenzy!” his dad yelled.

“I’m kidding, Dad!” William laughed.

Then Mum looked at William affectionately.

“I’m so happy you are wanting this party and sticking up for yourself. I know your friends are still on their quest to defeat the curse, but you need to do what is best for you, love.”

“Me too, Mum. I can’t wait to show everyone the statue and tell them about how I got accepted to the university,” William replied.

“I’m very proud of you! Anyway, everything should be ready by the time your friends get here,” she said.

“Awesome! Thanks!” William replied.

It wasn’t long before the doorbell rang. It was Brandon, Jeremy, and Daniel.

“Hey! Come on in!” William said.

"You look happy. I mean, that's good, but I'm not used to this much. Like calm down a bit, mate," Jeremy said, laughing.

"I have lots of surprises to share," William said.

"Oh? I'm waiting," Brandon replied.

"You will have to wait until everyone gets here." William chuckled. Brandon gave a vexed look, but that changed when he saw William's mum placing some appetizers on the counter.

"Brandon, if I remember correctly, yer the one that's always hungry." She laughed.

"Yes, ma'am, and I'm not ashamed of it either!" Brandon retorted.

"Well, here you go then. And save some for everyone, please," she said.

William's mum placed on the table some homemade shortbread, mini shepherd's pies, sausage rolls, and pecan bites.

"Wow! This is quite the spread, ma'am. You must talk to my mum, as she also goes crazy over guests," Jeremy said.

"Margorie? Indeed, laddie, I do." She chuckled.

The doorbell rang again. It was Christian, Judy, and Latrice. They walked in, and Judy looked around in amazement.

"Quite the winter wonderland you have here! Everything is so beautiful!"

"Did you see the lights outside?" William asked.

"Yes, but maybe you should turn them off or your lecky bill will be outrageous!" Judy replied.

"True. Dad already grumbles about the bills as it is," he said.

William hung up their coats and directed them to the food on the table. William's dad was watching American hockey and screaming at the television when his team wasn't playing right.

William was excited for his friends to open their gifts. He couldn't wait any longer!

"OK. It's time for all of you to open your presents!"

"Presents for us?" Latrice exclaimed.

"Dad. Is it OK for you to go yell at the television in the other room while we open presents, please?" William asked.

His dad rolled his eyes but already knew ahead of time not to say anything because he would hear the wife naggin' him.

"OK, all. Look for your name on the gifts," William directed.

Each of them looked and grabbed their gift. They sat and waited until William gave the next directive, since William seemed to be in charge.

"Please...open them!" William exclaimed.

They wasted no time ripping off the paper that surrounded their treasures. Everyone was in shock over their own gift. Christian received a men's Bible with a carrying case. Jeremy, an old 2040 BerraT mini collectible. Latrice, a fiction book called *The White Witch*. Judy, an acrylic paint set. Brandon, a ship-in-a-bottle construction set. And Daniel, a pass to the archaeological site in County Skye.

"Holy crap! How did you remember? I haven't done anything with archaeology in a long time, but it's something I still enjoy," Daniel exclaimed.

"I feel bad now. We didn't bring you anything, yet you took the time to think of us," Judy cried.

"Not so fast! Remember, we pulled names for Christmas. I just thought this would be a good opportunity to give William his gift from me," Latrice said, smiling.

William went to comfort Judy and then took the gift from Latrice. "This is so perfectly wrapped; I don't want to open it!" He opened the gift and it was multiple things: a mug that said 'Best History is Scottish History', a pen set, a leather binder with a calendar and lined paper, and a small wooden box that held an old compass inside. The engraving read: 'when you have lost your way, know it can be found through history that brings you back to present day.' William looked shocked.

"This is absolutely perfect! Thank you so much!"

"I thought you might like that," Latrice said.

William then says, "I know I'm not part of your crusade, as I call it, but this is all for you so just relax and just enjoy this day. Plus, I have more surprises to share!"

Everyone was grateful for William's thoughtfulness. They all did a group hug. Even Sunset wedged his way in and nudged his head on Judy's knee.

"My next surprise is this. I got accepted to the University of Edinburgh for history studies. I want to become a history professor," William said. He was grinning from ear to ear.

"That is brilliant, mate!" Daniel exclaimed.

"Congratulations are in order! You think your mum would let have some Buckfast wine?" Brandon asked. The group looked at Brandon like he was aff his heid.

William quickly replied, "Not a chance. Nice try, though. Ready for the next surprise?"

"Not sure if we can handle any more surprises," Christian said.

They stood up and headed to what would normally have been the guest bedroom. This room, however, was set aside for William's shields. Ever since he learned about Robert the Bruce as a young boy, he collected shields from that time and beyond. However, his parents outdid themselves this year. They bought at auction a bronze statue of Saint Michael from a museum that had recently closed in Glasgow.

"So what's the story on this?" Christian asked.

"I'm so glad you asked. I strongly hinted to my dad about Glasgow's Historic Museum closing and going to have an auction," William stated.

"Of course you did," Jeremy said sarcastically. William continued.

"Anyway, it was very odd that the starting bid was only £500, and no one but my dad bid on it. In order to have it fit in this room, we had to bring it in through the window. Trust me, it was quite the production."

"Is there any significance to this particular statue? I mean, it's in a glass case," Christian asked.

William was happy to oblige answering his question. "This stands approximately 180 centimetres and is made out of pure bronze. Saint Michael is holding an aegis shield with a cross on the front, etched in gold around the edges, which historically alleged to have been used to send satan out of heaven. His wings are in the downward position, indicating he has just completed one of God's missions. Of note, in the other hand, the sword is missing. That's probably why no one bid on it at the auction."

"Are all the rest of the shields in here real or replicas?" Christian asked.

"Most of them are real, like the pavise and buckler from the Middle Ages, but the black Viking shield, for example, is a replica," William stated.

Under each shield, William had made a small placard listing the name, era, and how it would have been used. Shield were used for blocking—some for the whole body and some only big enough to cover the chest. He had his own mini museum.

After supper, everyone was pure done in. Daniel had to tell everyone that he was heading back to Edinburgh.

"William, thank you so much for everything." He glanced at everyone else. "I'm heading back to Edinburgh in the morning to spend Christmas early with Sabrina and my aunt."

Judy became concerned that he wouldn't return for Christmas at the community centre. Daniel voiced that he would be back in time for Christmas with them. He saw the relief Judy had on her face.

Latrice wanted to mention that she was casing the white book.

"Well, for those that are deciding to stay around, tomorrow I'm casing the white book."

Jeremy was confused by the announcement and replied, "You're putting a book in a box. Who cares?"

Latrice had a slight grin and replied, "It's put in a glass case, and I will cast a spell so it can't get into the wrong hands." She looked over at Daniel. "Apparently it was in the wrong hands when Kristine found it."

Daniel was confused but too scunnered to argue or ask questions.

Brandon wondered why Kristine and Jacquelyn weren't there. "Speaking of books, where's Kristine and Jacquelyn with the golden tome?"

Latrice answered, "Jacquelyn is on a wee holiday, and Kristine is bangin' her head decrypting the tome. She's havin' a bad go with it. I was going to see if I can help her with the tome sometime before Christmas."

Judy asked William, "It might be odd to ask, but will you be joining us at the community centre for Christmas?"

William paused for a moment. He hadn't really thought about it, and he didn't want to let anyone down, but he was not sure how he still felt about seeing Anna. "I will strongly think about it."

As everyone went to their vehicles, Jeremy and Christian whispered to the others, "Are we taking bets on whether or not William comes to the community centre?"

Judy smacked Jeremy and said, "Really, Jeremy? Rude!"

He replied while shrugging his shoulders, "I'm just asking what everyone was thinking."

Judy gave in a return a snide look.

The next day, Judy, Brandon, and Kristine arrived at Latrice's house. Kristine had a tight grip on the golden tome and was her frustrated self. Latrice welcomed them with quick informalities because she wanted to work with Kristine before casing the white book.

"What did Samantha say to you about how to work the tome?"

Kristine sighed heavily. If she had to explain it one more time, she was going to burst.

"She basically said it will work when humility, compassion, and love are present."

Brandon definitely couldn't let this slide. His sarcasm got away with him.

"Well, that's it then! She's missing all three! Sorry, I couldn't resist. I'm just kidding, Kristine. Don't worry, we will figure this out!"

Both Judy and Latrice almost grabbed the tome away from Kristine to smack him with it. Latrice had to say something in return to his sarcasm.

"Now is not the time, Brandon. However, there could be some truth to what he said. If you don't possess all three, then the tome won't show itself."

Brandon wasn't sure what that meant and asked, "What do you mean not show itself? I see it right there in her hands!"

Latrice replied, "Oh, it means when she opens the book, the pages are empty. The words that we need to chant to the spirits will only show if you have the three attributes."

Brandon thought about it for a moment, then asked another question. "Then why don't you take it and get the words to show?"

Latrice nodded as it was another great question, and she answered, "The tome was entrusted to Kristine; therefore, she must find the way to read from it. Once she reads from the revealed pages, she will have to return it. This was a task given directly to her. Kristine must overcome whatever is blocking the attributes from coming together to reveal the words."

Judy didn't realise the pressure on Kristine's shoulders. She looked at Kristine with sadness and asked, "Is there anything you feel that would block your attributes from becoming whole?"

Kristine thought about it for a moment and assessed that love was missing. She told the story about when her mother died and her father wasn't present in her life. She'd been living with her brother, who was barely around because he went to the university and worked.

Judy placed her hand over Kristine's death grip hand on the tome and said, "You are one of my favourite people. With your fiery attitude and forthright demeanour, you are well appreciated in the grove. We all love you very much, and you have family in us."

Kristine looked at Judy with admiration and smiled back at her. She wasn't used to hearing the words *I love you.* Although Judy's words were kind, it still didn't feel the same as having actual family members love you. That would always be a void until she could accept it and accept love from her friends.

"I guess that is something I need to work on." Kristine looked at the book. "And fast if I'm to read from the book. I mean, no pressure, right? Just trying to free Beith, release spirits. Should be easy!" Kristine laughed.

Kristine opened the tome just to see if the pages were empty. However, this time, a few words showed. "Look!"

Brandon, Judy, and Latrice looked at the book, and a few words showed, then disappeared again. Latrice realised what was happening and reassured Kristine. "Whatever thoughts you just had to show the words, keep that up. You must have thought of someone and gave compassion and love. Or even humility, expressing to us what you have been holding in. You are doing great, Kristine. You will definitely be ready once everything is in place."

Brandon chimed in and said, "We are definitely here for you, and we all love you as our friend and our family. Both within the grove and just part of all of us."

Judy looked at Brandon with tears in her eyes. She put her arms around him and kissed him. Latrice saw them, and said, "Just stop, you two. Not havin' any of that now."

Latrice rolled her eyes and said, "OK, now it's time to case the white book. The one truthful thing Julia did say is that not knowing what you're doing or how to properly chant, call the spirits, et cetera, could cause more harm than good. This particular white book has to be studied.

It has unknown origins where many eyes have glared upon its pages and mouths possibly whispered it words. The risk is too high to have it out in the open. Therefore it's time to have it rest for now."

She placed the white book carefully in a clear glass case with white edges. Latrice chanted protection spells from both Druid and witch alike. When she cast the witching protective spell, golden symbols appeared on the top. However, only those that could see the symbols could open the case. Latrice looked at Judy, and without saying a word, Judy was able to see them. Latrice placed the case inside a perfectly shaped square hole behind her door. She then placed both hands over the hole, said a few inaudible words, and they all witnessed the hole seal. It looked as though the wall had never been touched. Latrice then gave further instructions.

"When the time is right, this and the golden tome will go back to the archives. Only there they will be safe."

Judy didn't feel right afterwords. She was confused as to why she could see the symbols. What plans did Latrice have for her? Latrice cast both Druid and witch protection spells, so how would she open the case?

Latrice saw the concern in her face and thought of an idea. "Brandon. Could you be a dear and get us some food from Nonna's, please? And take Kristine with you. I'll hold the tome until you get back."

Brandon looked at Latrice and figured she needed to talk to Judy. He and Kristine agreed and left. Latrice sat down and asked Judy to do the same. What Latrice was about to say, Judy was not prepared for.

"I sent them away because you have the right to know why I made it so you could see the symbols. Or runes. I was reluctant to use that term, but that's essentially what they are. Actual protection runes. There might be a time when we destroy the black book, and I could die. Now before you leap out of yer skin, listen. I can only do so much by myself, and I know the grove is here to help, but there are just some things I may not be able to overcome. Although in my absence, I would see you as the high priestess, you must involve the spirits in everything. All that I have done today is precautionary if my time becomes nigh."

Judy felt sick. She didn't know if it was from her being hungry or from what Latrice just said. Possibly a mixture of the two. But one thing was for sure—she didn't want to be high priestess nor be without Latrice. Then Judy fell to her knees and cried. Latrice just watched her. Although Latrice had sympathy for her, she had to allow Judy to extinguish the pain. One thing was for sure: Judy had a lot of compassion, humility, strength, and love, but it would be up to the spirits to determine her fate if it came to that.

Judy started to settle down a bit and wiped her tears away. Latrice gave a little tug on Judy's ponytail. They both laughed, then embraced and said, "I hope they hurry up with the scran!"

Latrice, Judy, and Brandon waited until nightfall to venture back to Julia's refuge. Nothing was eerie or seemed out of the norm. They took the shortcut from the car park to Julia's abode as mentioned from the last time they were there.

"I'm hoping she left us some clues," Latrice said.

"What kind of clues are ye lookin' for?" Judy asked.

"Anything really. Maybe who she's really protecting? Or something about the tomes? I'm not sure," Latrice replied.

They reached the area where the stones were. One of the 'Do Not Cross' tapes were still tied up to one of the trees. As they reached Julia's domain, Latrice asked,

"Does anyone remember how she opened it?"

"She pressed those stones simultaneously," Brandon remembered.

Brandon and Judy got on each side and pressed the stones. The floor moved. They looked down, and it was pitch black! Brandon flicked on his torch and headed first down the steep steps. Judy and Latrice followed, and when they were inside, the stone moved shut.

"That can't be good," Latrice said nervously.

"Let's just look around and get out of here!" Judy exclaimed.

Brandon flashed the light in every cravats he could find.

"Nothing!" Latrice yelled. "Let's get out of here!"

Judy looked on the wall and there hanged Anna's baby picture. Latrice looked and went to take it off the wall but the moment she touched it, it faded into the darkness.

"Looks like that's an indicator she had planned her death all along," Latrice said.

"Well, maybe we can use this place for what it was originally intended for and help others," Judy said.

"Or use it as a get away for us if we need it. Make it special," Latrice added.

They looked around the area one last time before departing.

Brandon remembered having to press two other stones by the staircase. The large stone rolled open, and they swiftly went up the stairs. They watched as the stone closed then headed back home.

Chapter 11

PEACE AND GOODWILL TOWARDS THE DEAD

Beith was a community, not just a town. It was full of life, history, and family. It took pride in its accomplishments and loved taking pictures of events and special occasions. From wee yins to the elderly, all were involved with the community. Its councillor was also dedicated to Beith's well-being and would go to great lengths for the county's people. This Christmas was no exception. No stone was left unturned for the people of Beith and the returned.

The community centre was bustling with activity for about a week prior to the centre's Christmas celebration. Volunteers from neighbouring communities also assisted with decorating, donations, and providing vendors for the special day. Many of the wreaths were donated from Kilmarnock, candles from Glasgow, and lights directly from the king and queen. Even those who weren't affected by the shadow directly provided support by donating horses and carriages for rides around the town, putting up lights, cleaning, just anything that would make Christmas perfect.

In order to ensure the safety of the people and respect for the returned, festivities and vendors were only held outside. The street leading to the centre was closed so vendors could sell their goods. From Buckfast wine to Tennent's Lager to shepherd's pie to clootie dumplings, there was enough variety of vendors for people to tantalize their tastebuds.

The decorations outside brought mystical warmth to anyone looking at them. The driveway leading to the centre was lit by large white candles encased in silver and gold lanterns. Next to each lantern was a wreath on a lowered stand decked with white bulbs. Surrounding the centre were multicoloured lights that hung from every birch tree. Each lamppost was hung with either a bell or pine tree display adorned with red, green, and white bulbs.

On the building itself, each window was frosted, with its frame outlined by mini white lights and finished with a smaller wreath that mirrored the standing ones. On the main door, the wreath that hung there was so large it measured from one side of the frame to the other.

The gang was all there except for William.

"I hope William shows up," Judy said.

"Don't worry about it. Let's go eat!" Brandon replied. He put his arms around Judy. She loved how his big, strong arms kept her warm.

Jeremy was happy to see Daniel back. "How was your Christmas holiday with Sabrina and your aunt?"

Daniel didn't really want to talk about it since it was the first one without his whole family, but he obliged the friendly enquiry. "It was good. Auntie got me a new radio for the car; Sabrina got me some tabletop archaeology thing. I think I'm about to dig up a dinosaur. Auntie made a whole bunch of food, and we talked. Sabrina pulled me aside and told me how Kristine stole the white book from her." Daniel chuckled. "Kidding, but she understood why. We just didn't tell Auntie, or she might have had us go to church three times a day."

Jeremy replied, "Glad you had a great time."

Judy's stomach growled, and Brandon looked at her funny. "Can't have my woman starvin'! Let's see Ms. Nancy at her truck."

Jeremy was happy to join the group in supporting the vendors rather than his mother doing her typical spread.

"Hi, Ms. Nancy! Can I get a cran-orange scone, a mini pie, and hot cider, please?" Judy asked.

"Of course, love. That will be £12.45. John will get that to ye at the other window," Nancy replied.

Daniel walked up, and Nancy welcomed him with a huge smile.

"Oh! It's so good to see you, Daniel!"

"Good to see you too! Ah, when did you start"—looking at the sign—"Nancy and John's Goodie Bar?" he asked.

"Just a few months ago. We needed something new and challenging. John is going to retire soon but is still a busybody. So here we are!" she said. Daniel laughed a little bit.

"You agree with that, Mr. John?"

John grinned.

"Do I have a choice?"

"So what would you like?" Nancy asked.

"I'll get the same as Judy," Daniel replied.

"Absolutely, love. John will have it ready for ye at the next window," she said.

The group sat on the benches behind the food trailers under one of the big birch trees.

"Oh my gosh! These are so good!" Judy exclaimed, holding up her mini shepherd's pie.

"Tell me about it! I might go back and get another order!" Daniel agreed.

"Brandon might get two or three more." Judy laughed.

"You're not speakin' far from the truth, my little love muffin," Brandon replied, pressing his nose against Judy's cheek.

"Wheesht, you two. We're tryin' to eat here! And don't start that snoggin' either," Latrice said.

Judy and Brandon kissed a little, and Judy replied, "You're just jealous, High Priestess! I have the cutest and best bard in all of Scotland!"

"Is he really, though? Can he play the bagpipes like the Royal Regiment we saw in Glasgow?" Latrice challenged.

Jeremy and Christian widened their eyes and weren't going to interject themselves into this conversation.

"OK. Maybe not as well as the regiment, but I'm pretty decent," Brandon stated, priding himself a little bit on his abilities.

"Let me guess. 'Amazing Grace' is your specialty," Latrice fired back.

"Yes, actually! It's the first song you play when learning the bagpipes," he replied.

"Noted. You may want to dust off your pipes as we get closer to hopefully releasing the dead," she said.

"Do we really need to discuss strategies right now?" Daniel asked.

"No. I was simply makin' a statement because the time will be soon. So enjoy all this while you can because we won't know the outcome after the destruction of one book to embracing the other," Latrice said.

"Speaking of which, where are Kristine and Jacquelyn?" Judy asked.

"Remind me to tell you later. She has to work on a few things internally," Latrice stated.

Judy looked puzzled and in disbelief and thought Kristine was working on her attributes.

"Like I said. Later," Latrice said.

Brandon jumped up and announced, "Time to get more plates!"

"See? I told ye!" Judy chuckled.

Latrice shook her head and smirked. She remembered one of the first times Judy and Brandon had stayed at her house.

"Remember when you and Brandon were at my house and had to get my auntie to make more popcorn because he ate both of ours?"

"Of course, I do! I was trying to watch an old Batman movie with a totally hot actor. I forget his name, but he was hot nonetheless. Brandon was tryin' to eat ye out of house and home!" Judy replied.

"Yep! And nothing has changed!" Latrice laughed.

Christian was looking around and noticed William walking towards the driveway. He called out to him and whistled so loudly that he could have hailed a cab from the north side of Beith.

Jeremy said while he covered his ears, "Thanks. Now that I'm deaf."

William heard Christian and gladly joined the group.

Christian and William greeted each other with a manly hug. Everyone else said their hellos.

"Did you eat already? If not, go see Ms. Nancy! Everything on her menu is great!" Judy confirmed.

"Maybe later. I just finished eating," William replied.

"You mean you don't do second and third supper like Brandon clearly does?" Latrice said, pointing at Brandon. The group chuckled. Brandon didn't mind the group pullin' a mickey on him.

"After Brandon finishes all his meals, we're heading inside to see the decorations." Christian paused. "And see Thomas and Anna. You up for that, mate?"

William sighed. "I have to put this behind me at some time; might as well do it now. But that doesn't mean I'm part of your adventures. Although I don't mind being kept in the loop."

"Well, that's good enough for us!" Daniel said. He gave a warm pat on William's back.

"We appreciate it. You were a huge help in finding the black book," Latrice said.

"Yeah. Never again. So don't ask. Not dealin' with books or birds," he replied.

"You ready, Brandon? No food allowed inside," Daniel explained.

"Ready!" he replied.

The group started walking towards the centre. Although it had been a joyous night thus far, the closer they got to the door, the more the tension set in. No one would say it, but everyone was worried about what William would do when he saw Anna. The guys kept close to William, while Brandon kept Judy as close as he could. They got closer, then William just stopped. Many thoughts were running through his mind as well. He remembered when he kissed Anna for the first time. He wanted that again but knew it was impossible now.

"You got this, mate. We are all here for ye," Daniel said.

William looked at Daniel, trying to stop the tears from falling. He shrugged off his feelings, cracked his knuckles, and said, "You're right. Let's go."

As they approached the main entrance, the elves smiled as they opened the door. "Please use quiet voices in respect for our returned family members."

"Of course, elf Jason." Judy chuckled, then looked at Brandon. "He's in my physics class." Brandon returned a smile.

William thought, *Returned family members? It was respectful, but the added smile made it sound like their return was acceptable. It's not!*

As the group walked in, they were met with immediate warmth and beauty.

"This is beautiful! It reminds me of your house, William!" Judy exclaimed.

"Thanks, but I think the councillor and other people really outdid themselves. Don't tell my mum that, though. This is really amazing," he replied.

In the corners inside the centre were decorated, four-foot Christmas trees in silver and gold. Next to them were placards describing the school and grade that had decorated them. Tables were set up in the main room with either green or red tablecloths and white runners, with a centrepiece of green garland with mini silver balls and a tall, battery-operated candle.

They had to look at the bigger tree from a small distance because a family was sitting at a table in front of it.

In front of the bay window stood an eight-foot tree that Councillor MacDannels and the children of Beith had decorated. Garlands of popcorn and coloured beads wrapped around the tree, along with coloured lights. Children from different schools and clubs had adorned the tree with their holiday ornaments made of paper and stained glass, in stars, bells, and other geometric shapes. Lastly, on top was a white-and-gold praying angel. Beith needed prayer due to the current situation, but no one was thinking about that. It was about right now. This moment of love and hope that filled the hearts of many. People knew that soon their loved ones would go, and all this would become future comforting memories.

"Our table is over here. My mum put in a special request," Jeremy stated.

They sat at a long rectangular table with a green tablecloth and a white runner. When they all sat down, they noticed there were only seven chairs.

"I'll stand once Anna and her dad get here," Jeremy offered.

While they waited for Anna and Thomas to shuffle in, the door was opened to the garden area. Because only one family group was allowed at one time, one or two people could stand in the doorway.

Judy quietly got up from her seat and said, "I'm going to go take a ganger."

"I'll go with ye," Latrice said.

There were times walking in the centre seemed like a traffic jam. The dead always had the right of way. You would have to stand, not make eye contact, and let them shuffle through. For Judy and Latrice, they had to stop and wait for one of the returned to shuffle through. One stopped right in front of them, looked at Judy and Latrice, then continued forward. Once their area was cleared, they were free to walk.

White lights were draped from one side of the dome to the bay window and the door. The small bridge was lit by smaller lanterns of silver and gold. The pond and the narrow river had floating lily pads with a battery-operated candle and different-coloured flames.

Judy and Latrice noticed the subtlety and elegance used to not startle the dead.

"I wish the dead or the returned knew how much we have done as a community for them. We meaning the town of Beith as a whole," Judy stated.

"We may never know. Come on. Let's get back," Latrice said.

Walking back to the table, they noticed Thomas but no Anna. They looked at each other.

"This can't be good," Latrice said.

"Dad. Everyone is here. Now where is Anna? Is she not having a good day?" Daniel asked. His face was flushed with worry.

Thomas looked at Daniel, his hands fidgeting in his lap. All eyes were on Thomas, and he felt the anticipation hovering over him like dark clouds preparing their storm.

In his stuttering, whispering voice, he said, "What I'm about to tell you is shocking, and you must remain calm so you do not upset the others." He leaned into the table. "Anna was taken. I had no way to get a hold of you, and I had to focus on some that were startled by the holiday preparations."

Christian whispered to Jeremy, "Great. William is going to become unglued."

"Too late," Jeremy replied.

William wasn't making a sound, but streams of tears flowed down his cheeks, his eyes were bloodshot red, and his facial expression was one of complete despair.

Looking at Daniel, he pointed to William. "Who is that?"

Daniel looked at William with concern. His heart was breaking too. Then he replied, "That's William. Anna's boyfriend. Or better yet, he would have been your son-in-law."

Thomas looked at William. "Come here, son."

William slowly got up from his chair, wiped his face, and walked over to Thomas. Thomas opened his arms, and they embraced in a long-standing hug. The whole table was either wiping away tears or fighting to not show them.

Thomas and William looked at each other, and William confirmed what Thomas already knew. "I loved your daughter so much."

"I believe you," Thomas replied. He smiled, then motioned to William to sit back down.

"So, Dad, how was Anna taken?" Daniel asked.

Still using his whispering voice, he replied, "It was after you left. We were walking towards one of the back rooms, and Anna stopped and pointed at something, but for me, there was nothing there. For her, she saw a demon in gold. Apparently this demon came towards her, she growled, then from what I did see was a purple inferno. They walked through it and vanished. I haven't seen her since."

Daniel looked at Latrice. "We have tae find a way to set them free. The sooner the better."

"Agreed," Latrice replied.

"Have you any information about how long we are to be here?" Thomas asked.

"Well, we have all been on quite the journey. I talked to Mum. She told me about Julia," Daniel started.

"Yes. So you now know that Anna is your cousin," Thomas replied.

Latrice was full of rage. She stood up, and in a loud whisper asked, "What else aren't you tellin' us, Thomas? You knew all along and made it out like it was some sort of mystery?! How dare you!"

"Latrice! No! Please!" Daniel pleaded.

"Merry freakin' Christmas, ye dobber!" Latrice said. She put on her jumper and left.

"Shite! Her face is like a skelped erse!" Jeremy stated.

Judy started to get up from her chair, but Brandon stopped her.

"Let her be for now. She needs time because she's under a lot of pressure to save Beith. I don't blame her for being upset."

Judy sat back down and watched the door, hoping for Latrice to return. Daniel looked back at Thomas, and asked, "Dad, what else do you know?"

There was a long pause. So long that the group was wondering if Thomas was going to talk to them again.

"I know that Julia killed your mother recently. I knew your mother really wasn't a high priestess, and because I held that secret for so long, I definitely deserve to die."

"Oh, I'm sure not goin' tae tell Latrice that," Jeremy whispered.

"Did you know about the altar? That Mum had dealings with the shadow?" Daniel asked.

"She had mentioned it, but I had no idea what she was goin' on about. I thought it was her Druid stuff," Thomas replied.

Thomas stood up. Then Daniel stood up and went to give his dad a hug, but Thomas pushed him away.

Daniel looked at him with trepidation, scared that he wouldn't see his father again.

"Dad, please. I love you. Don't push me away!"

Daniel held out his hand. He didn't care anymore about the altar, the dead, his mum. He wanted to reassure his father that he was forgiven and never forgotten.

Thomas slowly reached for Daniel's hand, placed it upon his cheek, and smiled. He let his hand go gently and shuffled away. Daniel watched in tears as his father staggered down the lightly dimmed hallway until he turned the corner and disappeared. Daniel stood, hoping that his father would change his mind and return, but it didn't happen.

Brandon whispered to Daniel, "Come on, mate. It's time to go."

As they walked past the table in front of the big Christmas tree, Judy watched as the family with their returned smiled at each other. The returned pointed at the candle on the table and stuttered, "Christmas." The family quietly applauded and went back to their smiles. Judy was full of tears and wanted that so much for Daniel and William. Judy looked back in hopes of catching a glimpse of Thomas, but he was not there.

The group went outside and looked for Latrice. They walked down the driveway and noticed that she was on the bench greetin'. Brandon suggested that Judy go to her. Judy, seeing Latrice broken because of the weight she had borne, she replied, "She had all this put upon her. She needs all of us."

They sat on the bench next to her, gave her a hug, rubbed her back, and told her they loved her. Latrice looked up at them and smiled a little. Ms. Nancy heard them and brought out a tray laden with hot cider. She didn't keep tabs on the teens because it reminded her of Agnes. Yet these teens had been braver than any knight, and they deserved any and all support. Ms. Nancy turned to walk back, but Latrice stopped her.

"Ms. Nancy, you can stay."

Nancy went to grab her jacket and returned. Latrice decided to tell the group what was coming.

"I'm sorry. I feel selfish for feeling like everything is on me."

"No one feels—" Judy started but was interrupted by Latrice.

"Let me finish. Please. We all have played a part in saving Beith. I wonder where the half Druid and witch adults are. From what I know, they're dead. Here is what I do know. Kristine is having a difficult time with the tome. She was trusted with it but can't read the words because it's empty to her. If she can't read the book in time, the spirits won't be freed, and the dead will remain. Secondly, when we destroy the black book, due to its power, it could cause an adverse effect and bring something nefarious and more powerful than me. We don't have much time left and are only hanging on one plan to work. So I'm feeling a little on edge."

Ms. Nancy sat down, and said, "I know I have been away from all of this due to your mother"—she looked at Daniel, then back at Latrice—"and I think many of us in Beith don't understand the severity of the situation or frankly believe it."

Brandon said, "The time where they brought in bulldozers to clear out the area so we could eventually bury the altar."

Judy said, "The councillor is a huge help, and think about all the other people even outside of Beith, like Samantha in Edinburgh. Oh, and Ms. Irene allowing Kristine and Jacquelyn to stay at her house."

Latrice said, grinning, "And when Ms. Margorie provides food for us when she doesn't have to." She looked at everyone and continued. "They may not understand fully, but Beith has our back, and we need that more than ever now." She looked at Ms. Nancy. "And we have Ms. Nancy to bring us hot cider!"

Nancy replied, "My pleasure, loves."

Judy put her arm around Latrice and asked, "Are you better now?"

Latrice tilted her head on Judy's shoulder, and said, "Yes, and I have one more thing I have to do before we destroy the black book." She sat up, and said, "I have to tell the councillor what is needed to properly release the spirits."

Christian asked, "What is needed?"

"A crematory," Latrice replied.

Councillor MacDannels agreed to visit with Latrice. He needed an update on the returned anyway.

Latrice walked through the door and was welcomed by Ms. Margorie.

"Hello, Latrice. The councillor is ready to see you."

Margorie opened the door and gleefully acknowledged, "She's here!"

Councillor MacDannels waved her in and said, "Margorie, no interruptions please. Just take notes for me."

Margorie responded, "Yes, Councillor." She smiled at Latrice and closed the door.

He looked at Latrice nervously. "You sounded distressed over the phone. You must have news to tell me."

She settled herself in the chair and proceeded to tell him about the golden tome and black book. "If we can have the roads blocked off by the warehouses, that would be most helpful."

He interlaced his hands together and looked at Latrice intently. "Now what is this matter about a crematory? We have one with six bays. How is this going to work? And will it be respectful in any sort of way?"

"This is what I hope will happen. Once we destroy the black book, we will use an ancient tome in hopes of releasing the spirits from the netherworld. It is two separate ceremonies, for lack of a better term. In order to ensure we don't have another incident like this again, if all works like it should, the dead will actually die and will then need to be taken to the crematorium. I think it would be proper to have the community decide what they wish to do with their families ashes."

"I think that's a brilliant idea, and yes, I hope all this works out well. Thank you, Latrice. May your spirits guide your path. I do hope that was the correct verbiage," MacDannels said.

"That is sweet, Councillor. Yes...yes it was," Latrice replied.

Chapter 12

FREE TO FLY LIKE GOLDEN EAGLES

A few days after the Christmas celebration, it was time to destroy the black book. The day before, rain and snow had lasted all day and saturated the ground. Latrice wasn't sure how things would have panned out had they tried yesterday.

The book of all evils that helped take away the innocent would now hopefully, once destroyed, open the door to free the dead's spirits. Once the black book was destroyed, Kristine could use the golden tome to release the spirits.

"We only have one chance at this, so let's ensure everyone is where they need to be. Judy, you call Christian and Brandon to meet the councillor at the community centre. Daniel, make sure the crematorium is ready," Latrice directed.

"The crematorium is ready. They did say they have a total of six chambers, all staff is present, and it will take approximately three hours to process each body," Daniel reported.

"Christian and Brandon just arrived at the community centre. Looks like everyone is in place," Judy stated.

The local police had taped off the road leading to the warehouses. Of course, there were other ways to get around, like going through the wooded area to the east. Thankfully, it seemed no one had tried that route.

Jeremy made a large round raised pit of wood and stone. He lit the pit, and a roaring fire of blue and orange engulfed the edges.

"It's time," Judy said.

"I wasn't going to say this until now, but for all your safety, I have to do this alone. Essentially I'm the only witch here," Latrice announced.

"We are not going anywhere. We are all here for you and will protect you," Daniel exclaimed.

Latrice watched the ravens dance around the warehouse as though they were celebrating a jubilee. They kept a keen eye on the group, cawing loudly as if sending encrypted messages to one another. It was as if they knew what was coming.

All were present except for William.

"William wishes us luck destroying the creepy book," Jeremy said.

"Whatever," Latrice responded.

"What's your problem?" Daniel asked.

"I get it, but..." Latrice started. She shook her head in disbelief. "Doesn't he think the rest of us are freaked out as well? He's supposed to be our friend! We are in this together! Aren't we?"

"I get how you feel. But let's face it. William really has no connection to this whole situation except for Anna. He's not a Druid or a witch. His mother didn't play with demons to get souls like mine did, and he had no family members taken from the shadow. Yes, he mourns for those we have lost, but his circumstances are different. You have to accept that. Not everyone has experienced what we have," Daniel explained.

"Well, I guess when you word it like that. I"—she looked at everyone—"I mean, we accepted William as part of our group. I don't know," Latrice responded, not sure what to say.

"William is still part of the group, but Daniel is right. We have to have compassion for each person's situation, whether we agree with it or not," Judy added.

"Fine. It's time to begin," Latrice responded.

Latrice took the black book and moved closer to the pit. Judy, Daniel, and Jeremy moved beside her but not too close, as instructed. Latrice ripped the first page and put it in the fire. One of the raven's cawed, then flew away. Judy, Daniel, and Jeremy looked at each other, thinking this was a good sign. Latrice ripped another page and put it in the fire. Then another page, and another. Soon Judy glanced at Latrice and noticed the tri knot tattooed on her neck was now glowing purple, and dark purple veins were protruding from her chin and past her neck.

Judy tapped Daniel and pointed to Latrice's neck. Daniel tapped Jeremy and did the same.

"Do we interrupt her, or do we stay quiet?" Jeremy whispered.

"I've been wondering why you've been so quiet. All I'm doing is burning a book," Latrice said.

"Well, it might be a little more than that. Your tattoo and the veins in your neck are a dark purple. So yeah, that's a bit scary," Jeremy said.

Latrice didn't respond right away, but she knew things were going to get worse. It was only a matter of time before she would capitulate to what might come from the fire.

"I don't know what will happen, but it is best that you move away. Soon I may not be able to respond at all," Latrice said. Her skin turned pure white, and the dark purple veins looked like dead branches creeping up on her neck.

The black book was more than halfway torn away, and the fire started to rise higher.

"Stay strong, Latrice! Remember, you are a warrior!" Judy yelled.

Latrice continued to rip the pages out and put them in the fire. She only had a few pages left when her eyes turned black, and she screamed, "You can't control me!" Her voice changed, like she spoke like demons. A conspiracy of ravens flew off after hearing her voice, but many still remained. Cawing. Some came closer and pecked at her hand, making her hand bleed. The blood caused the ground around her to decay. Latrice got down to the book's binding. She threw it into the fire, and the fire rose higher than ever at that point.

Just when Daniel and Jeremy went to pull Latrice away from the fire, a tall demon with six red eyes and a tall golden crown emerged from the fire.

The demon spoke some inaudible words. He directed his hand towards Latrice's head in what looked like an action to drain her soul from her body.

"You can't have her!" Judy yelled.

He looked at Judy, and with his eyes, he threw Judy back, knocking her unconscious.

"A kelem a shal e dorae!" Latrice yelled. It was her last effort to fight off the demon, but the demon laughed.

"Give up and come be with me forever. You will have more powers than what you have here. Allow me to show you." When he went to place his hand over her head, he was blocked. The spell she shouted out was a protection barrier; however, she knew it wouldn't last as long as the demon was present.

While Daniel and Jeremy were trying to wake up Judy, a man with a shield ran towards them, jumping over the barrier and crashing the shield upon the demon, almost splitting him into two.

"Shite! That's William!" Jeremy exclaimed.

"No way! He's at home!" Daniel stated.

"Well, now he's here," Jeremy replied.

The demon immediately healed himself and grabbed William by the neck and lifted him off the ground. William still had a death grip on the shield and struggled to hit the demon again. Coughing and gasping for air while kicking and moving to break free were only failed attempts. The demon laughed and held him there like a puppet on strings.

This had lasted for a couple of minutes when the dark clouds parted, and the remainder of the ravens flew away. A powerful beam of light came straight down, freed William, knocking him to the ground, and severed the demon completely. The demon's mangled body turned to ash and blew away in the wind. The crown of gold and the gems and pearls therein all turned to stone. Worthless stone.

William, still holding the shield, looked up at the bright figure holding the sword. The figure gently took the shield and headed back to the sky. The beam of light was gone, and the clouds came back together as though they had never been disturbed.

"Judy! Judy! Come on, lass! Wake up!" Jeremy exclaimed.

Daniel ran over to Latrice.

"Latrice. Are you OK?" Daniel asked in desperation. He waited until she opened her eyes. Her eyes were back to navy blue, she had rosy cheeks, and the dark purple veins had disappeared.

William was still looking at the sky, and his hand was still locked in place as though he was still holding the shield.

"Someone is really going to have to explain to me what just happened. I'm not sure what was more terrifying: the demon or the light thing," Jeremy said. "You do realise none of this is normal!" he added.

"Latrice! You did it!" Daniel exclaimed.

She sat up and rubbed her eyes. There were a few lingering flames, but just a few stomps would get them out completely. Jeremy decided to take an extra precaution and piss on the flames.

"Well done, Jeremy! You saved the day!" Latrice said. Latrice, Daniel, and Jeremy laughed.

Jeremy zipped up his trousers and replied, "That's right! I'm here for you!"

Jeremy noticed William was still in shock. "Snap out of it, mate! It's over!"

"Did you see that? He took my shield!" William exclaimed.

"Who took your shield?" Judy asked.

"It had to be him. That's why the sword is not with the statue; it's because it was with him all along," William stated.

Judy dusted herself off and went to sit next to Latrice.

"You OK, love?" Latrice asked.

"Yeah, I'm fine. That demon knocked me back, but I'm OK now." Judy smiled.

"Mate! I think yer heid is oot the windae! I think you're in a wee bit of shock," Jeremy stated.

William replied softly, "You're right."

"I have an ambulance coming just to make sure," Daniel stated.

"Let the councillor know that we will do the ceremony after we are checked out. We need our strength, that's for sure," Latrice stated.

"Maybe we should rest today, then do the ceremony tomorrow," Judy requested.

"No! We are going to finish this! Let Kristine and Jacquelyn know we will be on our way after we are checked out!" Latrice demanded.

"Yes, High Priestess," Judy replied. Judy frowned a little.

It wasn't long before the ambulance arrived and took them to the nearest hospital. Nurses were on standby, waiting for their arrival.

Judy and Latrice were in separate rooms, each of them being asked the same questions multiple times by multiple people. Judy had a bump on her head but had no concussion. Her vitals were normal, and she was free to leave. Latrice, on the other hand, was having complications.

"It seems like your body went under heavy amounts of stress. Your blood pressure is high for someone your age," the nurse stated.

"If you were fighting a demon that was trying to suck the life oot of ye, you would have high blood pressure too! But I wouldn't expect you to understand, Nurse"—looking at her badge—"Catherine," Latrice exclaimed.

"I'll have you know that I grew up in Beith and moved to Kilmarnock at the age of ten. I didn't encounter what others are experiencing or experienced, but I understand it. And I understand what yer doin' is important for Beith," Nurse Catherine said.

"Is it OK to see my friends?" Latrice asked.

"Sure. I'll check your pressure again in an hour. If it's down, then we can let ye go," Nurse Catherine stated.

She smiled, then left. Not even a minute later, William and Jeremy walked in.

"Well? What did they say?" Jeremy asked.

"My BP has to go down before I can be discharged," Latrice said. She was absolutely irked with the whole idea of being there, but she appreciated Daniel's reasoning. She looked at William and showed a slight smirk.

"As for you, you cheeky bastard, what made you come to the warehouse?"

William wanted to reply as sincerely as possible. "To be honest, it wasn't the plan, but knowing how much that book creeped me out, I couldn't imagine what would happen if I didn't try to help. I looked at the shield in the glass case, and something told me to take it and go to you! I know you guys probably hated me for not being around much, but I tried to make up for it in my own way."

"Well, I hated you, but I don't now," Latrice replied.

"Yeah, she did!" Jeremy exclaimed.

"Shush it!" Latrice responded.

"That's comforting. I guess," William responded with uncertainty.

"We gotta think of a way to get Latrice out of here! Hmm, I think I have a plan!" Jeremy stated, then he continued. "Latrice! You are the best Druid/witch person we have ever known. That can save us and Beith in its dire need!"

"Yeah, she can," Judy said, smiling as she walked in.

"Keep going! I approve of this, Jeremy. You could be the next bard," Latrice acknowledged.

"Goodness no! Stop!" Judy exclaimed. "We don't want Brandon to think he has competition!" Judy laughed.

"And we don't want all these compliments going to Latrice's heid!" William said.

"Oh! You're one to talk, Mr. Historian," Latrice said.

They couldn't stop laughing. Although they all had just been through hell, the group always found ways to make light of the situation. To come back and be there for each other. Bonds that couldn't be broken, even by demons.

Nurse Catherine walked in.

"Sounds like a good time in here! Let take your blood pressure."

She took it twice because she couldn't believe it.

"Well, 99/75. You are free to leave. Just sign these documents and come back if you have any complications. Oh, and Ms. Beaumont"—Latrice looked at the nurse with anticipation—"thank you for all that yer doin' for Beith. May you one day have all the peace you deserve."

"Thank you," Latrice replied. She signed the release documents, and they all left to head to the grove.

"Judy, please text Kristine to let them know we are on our way. She and Jacquelyn should have everything ready," Latrice said.

"Brandon is on his way as well. He said that many people came to help and are anxiously waiting to see what happens next," Judy said.

"OK. Let's save Beith once and for all!" Latrice exclaimed.

They arrived at the grove. What the group saw was beautiful. Many townsmen had volunteered their time to have new logs put in for seating and a round, solid stone firepit in the centre. Latrice looked at the gentleman, and he said calmly,

"We know you have to do your business here, but me and a couple of gents got together to do this. I hope it's enough, lass." He was in an old flannel shirt and jeans, black boots, and a straw hat. Latrice felt so honoured and humbled at the same time. She gave the man a big hug while tears slowly trickled down her cheeks.

"None of that now, lass. No need for greetin'," the gentleman said.

"Thank you, sir. It's perfect," Latrice said to him. The gentleman walked back up the slight embankment to the road.

This time there were no fancy robes or hair pieces. There wasn't any time for that. Latrice hoped the spirits would approve considering all they had been through that morning. Time was of the essence! It was either today or never in accordance with the golden tome.

The attendees sat on the new logs while the ceremonial grove members got into position. On the north side of the circle stood Judy; on the west, Kristine; on the east, Jacquelyn; and on the south, Brandon. Latrice stood at the centre next to the pit. Judy began to speak. "As we move past our Winter Solstice, we come to the spirits asking for the release of spirits that are trapped in the netherworld."

"I, Jacquelyn, ovate of the grove, call upon the hawk spirit of the east. I ask for your wisdom and release of the spirits in the netherworld."

"I, Brandon, bard of the grove, call upon the wolf spirit of the south. I ask for your wisdom and release of the spirits in the netherworld."

"I, Kristine, ovate of the grove, call upon the salmon spirit of the west. I ask for your wisdom and release of the spirits in the netherworld."

"I, Judy, ovate of the grove, call upon the bear spirit of the north. I ask for your wisdom and release of the spirits in the netherworld."

"All-knowing spirits of the four corners, we ask that you hear our plea. With the release of dead and spirit, this will bring balance. I ask for your wisdom and for balance," Latrice said.

Kristine moved to the table while another member moved to her spot so the circle was not broken. When she opened the tome, the pages were blank. She carefully flipped through the pages, and all of them were blank. Kristine panicked and shut the book. She looked around and noticed a woman coming down the hill wearing golden robes. Only an Arch Druid could wear that colour.

The Arch Druid walked slowly towards Kristine and the golden tome. The woman stood next to Kristine, and Kristine gently moved the tome towards the woman's direction. She opened the tome to its rightful place within, and words started to appear. Kristine's eyes widened in amazement but also bewilderment as to why the book didn't show anything to her.

"Spirits of this grove, I, Samantha, Arch Druid of Kalezak and grandmother to the fallen, ask for your forgiveness, wisdom, and release of the spirits." Samantha paused and then read from the book, "'As to the sun as to the earth, thus will turn and give life from birth. Evil comes and will not prevail, for our faith in spirit of the east, south, west, and north, we bow to you and will not fail. We come in humility and hang our hearts in shame; we did on our own, and death was the price we paid. Come to us now in your glorious wisdom and allow peace and balance to spread across this land again.'"

She closed the tome and sat on one of the logs. And now they waited. Their eyes were closed, and the ones that called out to their spirit waited until they were encompassed by the spirit, almost to the point of being in a trancelike state.

"Oh, Nixia? My dearest child. Look out to my dominion and what do you see?" the dark king asked.

Using her magic, she opened the velvet drapes and was happy to see the torture being inflicted on souls by the other demons. Then she looked to her right and saw many souls moving upward.

"Where are they going? I know I didn't release anyone! This cannot be!"

The dark king said sardonically, "Oh, but it is. The one we have been waiting for spoke from the golden tome, and we have nothing to hold them here. Now whose fault do you think that is?"

She looked at her father and replied, "The demon that we set on fire, my father."

He pointed his finger in the air and waved it back and forth, and said, "No, that is incorrect. It is yours!"

Nixia looked at him angrily and spouted back, "Not true! Had you let me go back to earth and retrieve it from those Druid brats, we wouldn't be in the situation!"

He knew what she was saying was true, but he didn't like it. The dark king was to never be crossed by anyone. Instead, he decided to deflect the situation and put it back on her.

"Had you not wasted a day to familiarize yourself with Beith, you would have had the tome in your possession. Again you disappoint me and are not worthy of my favour. You couldn't produce the tome; you couldn't get the name of the warder..."

Nixia interjected and surprised him. "I knew for a while that Samantha was the warder. She is Anna's grandmother and Arch Druid of her grove. I didn't want to tell you. You didn't deserve that!" She laughed uncontrollably and said, "I don't care what you do with me now."

The dark king grabbed her by the neck and made her blood boil. It was as though she were turned into lava. The melted body instantly cooled, and ash started to float up, then disappeared. Nixia was no more. No body. No soul. He looked at what he had done and roared, which resonated throughout his kingdom. Even Lilian felt her daughter's absence.

Jeremy received a text from Christian. *It's working!*

Jeremy wanted to scream it out but knew he shouldn't. He nudged the Arch Druid and showed her the text. She rubbed Jeremy's back and gave him an approving smile. The firepit radiated yellow and orange flames, indicating the spirits' approval.

The locals standing at the street above the grove cheered. They were hugging each other and yelling "thank you" to the Druids.

The grove swarmed around Samantha and immediately looked to her for needed answers. Kristine sadly looked at Samantha. She didn't need to ask because Samantha already knew what she needed.

"Kristine, love. Here, open it now." Kristine opened the tome, and all the words were there.

"How can this be?" she asked.

Samantha said with a smile, "At the beginning of the ceremony, you still couldn't see the words, but in your mind, you still showed compassion and love for your grove. You didn't receive humility until you reached out for help. No one else here could read from it but me. The ritualist told me to help any way I could."

Samantha looked at Latrice and knew her questions. "I will start by saying that I am the rune warder. I am Anna's grandmother. Secondly, before you can fully become a high priestess, you must ask the spirits to forgive the transgressions of the old and your own. You should be very proud of yourself and your grove. This was truly a gift from the spirits to allow you to get this far."

Latrice replied anxiously, "Will you come back and join us for the release of our loved ones? Can we come visit you? Will we see you again?"

Samantha said, "I did what I was called to do. It is now time for you to be blessed in this moment. And you know where to find me if you ever need me again."

Kristine exclaimed, "Wait! We need you to take the white book with you for safekeeping. Latrice will have to get it, though."

Latrice asked, "Samantha, could you please at least stay for one night so we can tell you about Anna? Jeremy's mum would be *honoured* to have you there and will cook up anything you like. Trust me!"

Samantha smiled. "I would love to hear about Anna. And I would be honoured to feast with you and your friends."

January 1, 2081. The days of Auld Lang Syne were behind them but not forgotten, and Beith had been restored. The day was cloudy, with a breeze that went from west to east, but no predicted storms. Everyone in Beith lined the loch's edge and waited for the councillor to start. It was no surprise that Jessica McGowen was present, waiting to show the world her latest big story. Before taking to the podium, Councillor MacDannels walked up to Jessica, and said, "I don't need a spectacle from you today. Something I should have told your mother but now tellin' you: for once bugger off and allow Beith to have their peace. This day is for them, not the world."

He turned around and walked towards the podium with a celebratory smile while Jessica and her crew departed.

"Citizens of Beith. Happy New Year! I am pleased to announce that thanks to our grove and many others that helped along the way, Beith is finally free!" People cheered and applauded. "I may have the authority to direct things, but there is one special young lady who actually did them. Latrice Beaumont, the high priestess of her grove, wanted to give a special thank you to all of you."

Councillor MacDannels motioned for her to come up to the podium, and Latrice looked at the crowd, who was looking at her. There was a long pause, but they waited patiently for her to begin.

"Hello. I did have a speech planned, but when I look out to all of you, you deserve more than pre-thought written words. I see a community that is founded on humility, compassion, love, and strength, and I was reminded not too long ago that these attributes work well when united. I have all of you to thank for our success in freeing our loved ones. I will not lie. I thought I was alone in this fight, but the citizens of Beith, the councillor, my grove, and the people from Glasgow and Edinburgh all had a part to play, and you played your part well. I speak for myself and my grove. We humbly thank you, appreciate you, and love you."

People cheered and wiped away some tears.

The councillor then introduced Judy. She would read the poem "Good Night, And Joy Be Wi' Ye A" by Alexander Boswell.

After Judy completed her recitation, there was much applause.

The councillor got back to the podium, and said, "One delightful person from Glasgow that some of you have already met is Father Mac. He is going to say a prayer for us, and when he's finished, you can open the urns and set your loved ones free. Father."

Father Mac took the podium.

"Thank you all for having me for this historic and monumental moment. From what I have learned, this community has suffered loss and deserves much peace. Today we don't remember how they died; we remember how they lived. Lived within our hearts, our community. How their smiles and their laughter brought us joy and comfort. Know that on this day, they will be within the light." He flipped the pages in his Bible. "A reading from the New Testament, the Book of Revelation chapter 21 verses 3–4. 'Behold, the dwelling place of God is with man. He will dwell with them, and they will be his people and God himself will be with them as their God. He will wipe away every tear from their eyes and death shall be no more, neither shall there be mourning, nor crying, nor pain anymore, for the former things have passed away.' The word of the Lord."

Brandon stood proudly in his full-dress Scottish attire and played his bagpipes the heart-rending tune "Amazing Grace."

Just then, rays from the hidden sun shone through the thickened clouds, and a golden eagle flew towards the north. When the families poured out the ashes, they could all see the heavenly splendour of the spirits that were once taken were now set free. People looked in amazement and were touched by its beauty. Even Father Mac couldn't believe his eyes but thanked God for his mercy and grace for the people in Beith.

The group stood next to Daniel as he poured out his father's ashes. They hugged him as the ashes fell into the water. When he finished, they looked up at the rays, but each of them was given a gift, a gift of seeing other family members sent to the light. Latrice covered her mouth, and tears flowed when she saw the spirit of her auntie Catlin. Daniel almost fainted when he saw Anna in all her beauty as he remembered her. Her spirit flowed like a soft breeze over to Daniel and William. She touched their cheeks and smiled. When she did, she was gone. Laurie floated up to Daniel and gave him a kiss on the forehead and he felt it through his heart. She smiled and disappeared into the sky. Not pieces of her but all of her.

Brandon finished and placed his bagpipes in the case. He walked over to the group and stood quietly. Rays of the sun were bouncing off a coin that laid in the sand. When Brandon picked it up, his eyes welled up.

Judy hugged him, and asked, "What is it?"

He turned the coin from front to back, back to front to ensure he was seeing the coin correctly. "It's my sister's. I'd know this anywhere." He looked to the sky. "She's with them too!"

They started to walk away, but Latrice stopped them. "Hold on."

They turned and looked towards the sky. She had to see for herself that every last soul embraced peace and would have eternal rest.

Kristine and Jacquelyn ran up to the group. Kristine said to Latrice, "I have all my attributes now."

Latrice still looking at the sky replied, "Ye, I think we all do now."

GLOSSARY

Scotland, England, Wales, and Ireland use certain words that many may not be familiar with. Also note that spellings are different as well, such as, using *-ise* versus the US using *-ize*, or using *-our* [favour] versus *-or* [favor].

Cannae – cannot
Daft – not very smart
Dobber – annoying; idiot; jerk
Eejit - idiot
Face is like a skelped erse/arse – [situational] ugly; red with rage; blushing
Gommy – simpleton; idiot
Greetin' – crying
Lassie/Laddie – girl/boy
Lecky – electric (lecky bill)
Manoeuvrability - maneuverability
Mate – friend
Mongo – derogatory for stupid
Partner – boyfriend/girlfriend; husband/wife
Peely-wally – not looking good; out of sorts
Scran - food
Scunnered – tired; tired of something/someone
Tae – to
Tatties – potatoes
Wee yin – small/little/young one
Wheesht – shut up
Yer bum's oot the windae. – You're lying or exaggerating
Yer aff yer heid. – You're going crazy

ABOUT THE AUTHOR

Kellyanne is originally from the Detroit Metropolitan area. She is an army retiree that served 21 years, has a master's degree in terrorism studies, and currently works as a government contractor in southern Arizona.

Writing provides a way for Kellyanne to relieve stress, gather her thoughts, and discover her own creativity. When not writing, she likes to be involved in her local church, play PC video games, and spend time with her two cats, Junior and Ollie.

Fun fact: Kellyanne grew up thinking she was Irish. She had a tattoo that said, "God blesses the Irish." However, when she researched her ancestry for a Father's Day project, to her surprise, the whole family was shown to be from Scotland. Eventually, she got a coverup tattoo of Scotland's flag on a shield blended with the Scottish thistle.

The family discovery, along with other influences, led to this particular book series.

Milton Keynes UK
Ingram Content Group UK Ltd.
UKHW011134220424
441551UK00006B/541